SAND DUNES AND WINDBLOWS

by

Agwuncha A. Nwankwo

First Published 1994
New Edition 2002 by
FOURTH DIMENSION PUBLISHING CO., LTD.
16 Fifth Ave. City Layout, P.M.B. 01164. Enugu. Nigeria email:
info@fdpbooks.com fdpbooks@aol.com,
Web site: http://www.fdpbooks.com.

ISBN 978-156-375-3

CONDITIONS OF SALE

Initial Cover design by Uche Ohagwu
Redesign by Ben Abanifi

Design and Typesetting by
FOURTH DIMENSION PUBLISHERS, ENUGU

Dedication

To

Philip G.E. Umeadi, Senior Advocate of Nigeria
Ozonma Na Nri

Chapter One

Bronx, New York

The meeting was held in the heart of Bronx, N.Y, in an underground cellar that was hacked out of a disused garage. Two shabby and weed-grown walls ran parallel to the front of the cellar, the approach of which was obscured by shambling tenement buildings. The ground beneath the walls was full of tepid sewer water, garbage and general refuse. The smell was thick and acrid.

Beyond the walls, towards 167th Avenue, the noise was always loud and perpetual: the roar of traffic, the juké-box music from the numerous shady night clubs, the screams of the injured on the roads and the raucous and shrill cries of street urchins who played with garbage cans and pick-pocketed on the sideline.

But once in the alley, the noise faded into a muted murmur, a babble of indeterminate echoes that hovered over the grimy landscape. At the end of the alley and very near the tenement, the noise petered out completely, only to be replaced by an eerie stillness. The last tenement building on the left had a trapdoor that served as its entrance. At the press of a computerised button, the trap door swung open to reveal the pressing darkness of a concrete-motorway. The motorway terminated at an immense space, large enough to hold about fifty cars. Several cars were parked there already; each belonging to different members of the consortium who were holding a meeting inside the underground cellar. Each car was sleek and of the latest model of their make. Each car had state of the art electronic gadgets and their tyres wore the marks of the sordid alley way, the only reminder that they did not belong to such squalid quarters.

The entire neighbourhood, right up to the houses on a half kilometre radius of the main avenue; was the property of the consortium, purchased within a period of ten years. The purchases had been systematically done, using different fronts and agencies that most of those who either lived, there or made their living in it had little or no idea that they paid their rent to the same concern.

There were some Italians, Spaniards and French nationals who were put up there through the connection of the members of the consortium. There were also Hispanics and Latinos who seemed to have settled overnight and who gave the neighbourhood its distinct colour and character. It was the same with the teeming black population that complemented the-international character of 167th Avenue and beyond. All these people owed their livelihood and existence to their friends and relations in high places who made their re-settlement and secure life possible. All of them were very loyal and passionately devoted to their benefactors. They were all prepared to lay down their lives for them. They were, so to say, all paid agents of the consortium, though they never f or once thought that they worked for the same masters.

The cellar was dimly lit. Subdued lights hung from wire baskets that seemed to spring out of the damp decking. They cast blunted shadows all over the narrow room, and particularly on the long table that dominated its centre. There were patches of brightness and gloom in the room; and some awful images. Except for the long table, the twenty-odd chairs and the people who were deep in discussion, the room was bare.

There were seventeen people inside the room, fourteen men and three women. They came from different countries and continents and each had a peculiar background but they all had one thing in common. They were the highest ranking members of the consortium, its principal actors and the motor of its numerous and sometimes vicious and ruthless machineries.

At the head of the table was Jack Edmonds, a tall, thin, wiry American whose leathery features and wash of glossy grey hairs gave the image of either a career diplomat or a respected professor of the sciences. But Jack Edmonds was neither a diplomat nor an academic. He was the Controller-General of the consortium, the brain behind its global operations. Next to him was a short, bulky man in his mid-thirties, whose fleshy face and very red lips betrayed his South African background. He was Caesar Leopoldo Oscar, a native Colombian who used as his operational headquarters, plush hotels in over thirty capitals of the world. He was smoking a cigar and had an animated glitter in his eyes. On his right was Escravor

Odaja, a Peruvian, a medium-sized man whose unnatural stillness gave one the impression of a deadly cobra. There was the Frenchman, Friedreich D'Armee; the Italian Angelo Ababos; the German Guttfried Von Guttlngberg; and the Polish Wojslav Jamicsz, who at his first teeth in the solidarity trade union movement as an enforcer, had fled his native land when he could not account for the millions of dollars that was passed to the movement by American industrial complexes, finance institutions and voluntary agencies through him.

Present also was the first lady of the consortium, Barbara Alvminea, half-dealer, reputed to have intimate details on over fifteen European heads of state; details which could even shock their wives. Already in her early forties, she still managed to appear breathtakingly beautiful and charming in her leopard skin two-piece suit with glittering sequins, diamond earrings and an enchanting perfume. The other two women were in their mid-thirties, resplendent in their designer's attire, and as ruthless and dedicated as their male colleagues. One was from Argentina and the other from Australia. There were also a sprinkling of Arabic and Asiatic types; two Sheiks from Oman and Kuwait, and three representatives of the Golden Triangle triad that stretched from Thailand to Taiwan, Singapore to Hong Kong, Nepal to Sri Lanka and Malaysia to Burma.

The High Command of the consortium knew the risk they were taking in converging at a particular place at once, especially in the very land that had sworn to exterminate them. In deciding to convene such a powerful gathering, they had two compelling justifications. One was their legendary confidence built over the years of careful planning and security management which earned them the passports of several countries; their mastery in the art of disguise and the desperate situation which they now must contend with, which a special committee could not resolve to their satisfaction. They had, therefore, come fully aware of the security implications of their gathering, but fortified by the belief that they must press on with the demands of their high agenda.

"Good evening, ladies and gentlemen of the consortium," Jack

Edmonds' voice rang out. "Before we embark on the deliberations of the day, may we observe a minute's silence in honour of our fallen friend, Pablo Escobar, who was recently cut down by the assassin's bullets. Pablo died in the cause of our struggle, at the very stage we were set to reveal our real selves to the world. He died from the bullets of cowardly local agents of darkness who were perennially goaded by the evil forces in America."

They observed the silence with impassive faces, save for Caesar Oscar, a long-standing comrade of Pablo who had roamed the wild forests of Medellin with him in their lucrative trade before he decided to make hotel suits his abode at the age of 23. There was a fierce glitter in his eyes. His mouth was rigid, with a momentary spasm that laced his cheeks and jaw lines.

"There are two business matters at hand today," Edmonds continued, "and I don't intend to waste your time. The first is the implications of the death of Pablo to the expansion of our business. The other is the political programme of action we must adopt in order to master the changing times."

He paused and scanned the faces around the table. Most of the men nodded. Others indicated that the agenda was okay with them. Nobody took notes. There was no paper available.

"The drugs war in Colombia is escalating every day and Pablo's death has made matters worse. Escobar wouldn't have died but for the betrayal by some elements in the Cali family. We need peace now, more than at any other time in our existence. I propose that a meeting of the strategic committee be convened in Colombia without delay to work out a peace agreement between the two cartels. We have already lost valuable men hi this senseless war; men and resources that would have helped to expand our base and frontier. -We need peace not for the markets that will open up; but peace in order to prosecute our political programme of action without delay."

"Peace is only possible in Colombia on -. One condition," Caesar Oscar said tensely, in a thin scratchy voice that was in sharp contrast to his bulky size.

"Most members of the cartels in Colombia-who are part of the consortium want peace. They crave and yearn for it everyday of their life. Only -two obstacles stand in the way of peace in Colombia Emmanuelos Des Animuos and the Colombia chief prosecutor. Nobody can make peace with the greedy Animous, and the chief prosecutor has sworn to exterminate any Colombian suspected of having any link whatsoever with our consortium. He is an agent of the American Government and is very much hated by most Colombians. Eliminate both men and there will be peace in Colombia."

As he spoke, Oscar sat very close to the table to communicate his passionate feelings to all those present. At the end of his speech, he sat farther back on his chair as a strange smile played on his lips. Somebody coughed around the table. Another sneezed discreetly into his dainty white handkerchief. Then the silence returned.

"Oscar knows the South American terrain very well," Edmonds resumed. "He is not called the master of the South -Seas for nothing. Does anybody have any objection to .his condition f or peace in Colombia?" A low murmur indicated that they went-along with his reasoning.

"That being the case, I. call on Odaja to set the contract arrangements without delay; and to see to the speedy resolution of this affair in as short a time as possible. The meeting in Colombia will convene in two weeks' time."

"We now come to the critical phase of our planning," the Controller-General, a graduate of Yale Business School, began softly. "A phase that will determine our place in the years to come; and a phase that will reveal our relevance in the coming century."

He stopped abruptly and clapped his hands. A slide panel opened and a tall man stepped out of the shadowy way with a pitcher of water and a glass cup. He wore an immaculate and well-tailored suit. His hair was oily and was plastered to his shiny forehead. His coat was open and his high calibre automatic pistol could be seen protruding from its holster. He walked up to the high table and placed the pitcher of water and retreated stealthily to the shadowy doorway. The panel swung shut.

"Ladies and gentlemen," Edmonds said, "the way to the future lies along the path of political power. We are overdue to take the world. This meeting will not resolve our political stand, but it can set our agenda. We have money. We have investments. We have economic power. We have got everything but there is something still lacking in our whole package: political power. There is virtually no government in the world we can call our own. This situation is unacceptable and must stop without delay. We spend billions of dollars yearly oiling the wheels of several governments, bribing legislators and ministers, persuading judges and influencing prosecutors. Half of this money can buy us power. Why waste a billion dollars on a rascally government that listens more to what Washington says when less than one quarter of that amount can put our agents in power in various countries. The time has, therefore, come when we must review our strategy. What I have in mind are as follows:

1. In the next six months, we will seize control of a key South American government, together with Mexico;
2. In the next one year, we should take control of Spain, Italy and Poland, including the Baltic Republics of Latvia and Estonia, a prime source and route of our expanding business;
3. In the same period, our Asian brothers should come out of the shadows and take what is theirs in Thailand, Malaysia, Nepal and Singapore.
4. We will leave America as our last target. Isolated by hostile regimes the world over, America will be a walk-over. I have plans for that; have had the plans for over a decade now."

He poured water into the tall frosted glass and took a rapid sip. He placed the glass on the table quietly and looked at his friends appealingly.

"You must be wondering whether I have lost my senses, and how possible it is for us to fight entire armies, cause social revolution and take political power. The time to do the mathematics on that is yet to come. The next one month will tell whether we have been fooling about or not. Don't forget that in some countries, we have stronger armed men than the governments' armies who spend their time protecting poppy fields, engaging in local feuds and raping-village women. Such sophisticated guards with the most modern weapons are not cut out for such lowly jobs. They must be productively engaged. However, I have the master plan to execute this programme; the only thing I require is your endorsement. The document which will contain the details of what I have in mind will be delivered to you all in four days' time, provided that you accept in principle my main thesis about the desirability of political power for the survival of the consortium."

The fourteen men and three women were speechless with admiration and fear. Most of them only had the basic education necessary to transact their very complex business. They were as far removed from politics as the sun is from the earth. They only wanted to live comfortably, have men over them, body-guards to bark at and women to use and abuse. This new theory enchanted and frightened them at the same time.

A few others were fully aware of the implications of their Controller-General's speech and. admired him for his vision and courage. They resolved to put faith in him while they closely watched how his plans would unfold.

The accent was very clear from the way everyone responded except for the moody countenance of Timothy Brown. Brown was the only African-American present at the meeting. Though unquestionably committed to the consortium, he had read a few extracts from the works of Frederick Douglas, Marcus Garvey, W;E.B. Dubois and Malcolm X. In each case, Africa was mentioned as the focal point, the spiritual heritage of all Blacks in America. Yet, their Inspired leader had no word on how to carry Africa along in his plans, how some African regimes could be toppled for their people to supervise the growth of the African market and future.

"Mr Chairman," he began, having resolved to make his views known, 'how about Africa? What plans do we have- for my black brothers there? When will the change come to those already destroyed by misrule under the instigation of Washington and -the other imperial masters?"

Jack Edmonds smiled at Brown's naivety. The others-watched closely and listened intently.

"Africa has only two strong links in our international transactions; Lagos, Nigeria, and Johannesburg, South Africa. Both links are fatally flawed. Lagos because of the unseriousness of the dealers and the moles and South Africa because of its' unstable political climate. Nigerian dealers are only given to buying flashy cars, marrying several wives and taking chieftaincy titles. South Africans are new in the trade. They cannot be relied on. In both instances, too, strong local organisations and cells do not exist; everybody operates as he deems fit. Africa will be left out of it for now."

Timothy Brown nodded understandingly. Jack Edmonds clapped his hands three times. Hidden panels opened behind all the people at the meeting and shadowy figures emerged from the dim recesses. They clutched the briefcases of their bosses and walked noiselessly towards the main entrance. The seventeen people remained seated for a couple of minutes and began to leave one after another at one-minute intervals, each taking a different route in his car

Chapter Two

Peter Nicholson was very worried. He had been worried since he was elevated the vice-president, International Banking and Corporated Finance of the First American Bank share. He had examined the relevant documents presented to him by his personal assistant and had broken out in sweat. What he saw disturbed him greatly. Large movements of capital across borders, guaranteed off-shore investments provided by questionable funds in their vaults and periodic and unverified lodgements of huge sums of money that apparently disappeared without a trace at odd intervals. Investigations had revealed that these numerous accounts were the innocuous fronts of a multiple accounting system that had thus far defied the expertise of the bank's auditors.

He had asked for an urgent appointment with the president of the bank, Anthony Roberts and specifically requested that they meet privately in the latter's personal chambers. The meeting took place in the president's penthouse in the bank's 49-storey imposing structure in downtown Manhattan.

Nicholson did not waste any time in coming to the subject and spoke passionately at length about - his tentative discoveries. He ended by telling the president: "My suspicion is that, contrary to established banking and financial procedures, and without the knowledge of the management of the bank, our institution has been regularly used for money laundering. My suspicion is that the money is drugs money."

Anthony Roberts sat impassively throughout his vee-pee's testimony, twiddling a-gold ball point in his well-manicured fingers. He occasionally looked out of the bay window that dominated the penthouse office and admired the flow of traffic and human activity down the boulevard which looked like a parade of ants.

"I wouldn't-have recommended you for the office of vice-president," he began when Nicholson had finished, "if I had any doubt about your capabilities and enthusiasm. The previous vice-president was, to say the least, incompetent and indifferent to such matters. Send in your report to me and be very discreet with your investigations. Will one week be enough?"

"Wes Sir," Nicholson replied, very pleased with himself. He left the office satisfied that he had accomplished a mission. However, he was taken aback by the president's comment that, he personally recommended him for the post of vice-president of international banking because that observation did not agree with the information-at this disposal.

He had it on good authority that his appointment was the result of boardroom politics and that Roberts was virtually compelled to accept it. May be, Roberts didn't really think highly of his abilities, but was not impressed with what he had discovered after barely a week in his new job. With a light heart and the promise of a bright prospect, he took' his leave and made his way to the corridor in search of the floor elevators that would take him to his 37th office. Soon after he left, Roberts picked up one of his telephone and spoke to the telephone operator: "Give me Nassau," he said. "I want to place an urgent call." He replaced the receiver on its cradle, left his desk and went to the bay window, a thoughtful look in his eyes, and a slight frown creasing his brow.

That was about a month ago, and nothing had happened to make Nicholson least worried; In fact, events had taken an absurd turn and he had the feeling of a man about to experience a terrible tragedy. He could not fathom out the source of his premonition but the feeling persisted. He had duly submitted his findings to Roberts and waited for action to be taken. None had come. Roberts' only comment when the document was presented to him' was to enquire whether he had made copies of his report. Nicholson was taken aback. He informed Roberts that he had two separate copies, one which was securely locked in his office safe and the other which he intended to present to the bank's board at their next meeting.

"That will not be necessary," Roberts had told him. "Your safe may not be quite as secure as you may think and who knows whether there is anybody on the board who may be behind some of these irregular operations. Such scale of fraud would not be possible unless somebody at the top is in the know. Bring all 'the papers to me and I will take care of everything."

Roberts smiled re-assuringly to him as he made these remarks, and though he was somewhat disturbed, he reassured himself that the president meant well. He duly returned all the documents, including the rough draft of his initial findings.

He now sat behind his desk staring into space and wondering about what next to do. Just a few days ago, over half a billion dollars was surreptitiously deposited in the bank's vaults and by yesterday, half the sum had already been dispersed to various corporations and industrial concerns. He wondered why. Suddenly, he made up his mind about what to do. He had to start all over again, quietly reconstructing his findings, which he would send personally to the board, no matter the consequences to his job and prospects. He would start tomorrow. Once he made that decision, his face lifted and the glow came back to his eyes.

He reached for the intercom on his desk and pressed the buzzer. His attractive secretary came into the room with a pad and a ball point. He smiled sweetly at her. "Cancel all my engagements tomorrow. I will be working here in the office. Cancel all my appointments, except perhaps, if the president or any of the board members requests my attention."

"Yes, Mr Nicholson," she answered and left the office.
Nicholson reached for his briefcase which was lying by his feet and lifted it to the desk. He selected some documents and put them inside the case. He snapped the locks and placed it again by his feet. He went to the coat rack and put on his well-tailored coat. He came back to the desk and lifted his briefcase from the floor. When he got to the door, he glanced at the desk again, and, satisfied that he had left nothing behind which he would need at home, left the office and clicked the door shut.

At the garage down-stairs, he unlocked his car and dumped his briefcase on the back seat. He drove out of the garage and headed for the main road. He never saw the black, beat-up dodge that came out of the garage with him and never suspected that it was just a couple of meters behind him.

He stopped at the traffic light, mindful only of the mission he had set his mind to accomplish. The dodge stopped about two cars behind him. When the light turned green he moved again and took the next intersection on the left that would take him to the residential pert of Manhattan. Trees lined the boulevard, casting shadows on the leafy road. He increased his speed. The dodge remained behind him.

He took another left turn and slowed down. The dodge slowed down too. A right turn brought him to bib street, a stretch of well-kept avenue with mostly single storey buildings with well-maintained lawns and brick wails. The gate to his house was open. He had no gateman, and his wife was away to work. The children would be in school. He had left the office very early. He looked at his wrist watch. The lime was 12.33 p.m.

He drove into the compound and parked the car in the open garage. His neighbourhood was a quiet and peaceful one and had the reputation of having experienced no petty robberies in the last three months.

As he pushed the key into the keyhole, there were shadows behind him on the lawn. He looked back and saw three men looking intently at him. Each wore a black suit. Each had a scarf knotted on his thick neck. Each had his hand inside his inner coat pocket.

He stood frozen and stared at them dumbly. "What can I do for you?" he managed to ask. They gave him a sinister smile.

"Nothing, Mr Nicholson, nothing," one of them said. "The consortium sends its love." Their hands flew out of their pockets and- the shinny muzzles of three automatic pistols pointed at him.

He saw that the gate had been shut. He opened his mouth to scream as the bullets tore into him. One shot caught him on the temple, another blasted the veins in his neck. The third pierced his heart. More bullets rang out dully, making the shallow noise of a tired clap. His briefcase slid out of his hand and rolled down the concrete steps that led to the front door. It snapped open, and his papers spilled out. His body began its bumpy descent until it lay beside the open briefcase.

The three men took one last glance at his still body, made their way rapidly to the gate which they flung open, and shut again when they were on the other side. The sound of a starting car was heard. Then silence returned to the neighbourhood, save for the thin roar of traffic on the main Manhattan boulevard.

* * *

Peter Roberts had been expecting this particular call since early afternoon. He moved restlessly about his office, his hands clammy and his chest heaving. He had been repeatedly reassured that everything would be okay, and he had nothing to worry about. Though such words should have calmed his frayed nerves instantly, coming from such a source whose power he knew so well, he had some foreboding.

The shrill sound of the telephone receiver intercepted his reverie abruptly. He dashed to his desk, snapping the receiver off the hook as he did so.

"Yes," he spoke softly. The voice at the other end was measured and totally at peace with itself.

"Why do you worry over little investments?" it began. "The shipment of the snails was delayed because their shells had to be broken open. However, they have arrived at the port. All of them, without their shells. Arrange for immediate delivery. Good day."

Roberts replaced the receiver gingerly. He mopped his forehead with his handkerchief. He felt not at ease or satisfied at the elimination of his immediate problem.

Other problems could still emerge and he wondered whether the millions he was being paid would compensate for the crunch he knew would come some day. Already, a few of the auditors were beginning to get suspicious about the movement of money in and out of the bank. They may be after him before long unless he became more careful.

Though he had been repeatedly reassured that nothing would go wrong, and he had no reason to doubt his masters, he still harboured the fear of an impending danger. He reached for a small bottle of Scotch he normally kept at hand, and took a swig. Emboldened by the Whisky, he forgot his fear and set about readying himself for his next engagement.

13

* * *

They met in a discotheque off Manhattan's 76th Avenue. The entrance to the dance hail was filled by young people in outlandish garbs, all waiting to get in. Neon lights flashed off and on and the sound of dance hail music could be heard faintly from the frosted glass swing door. Roberts waited for his turn.

Once inside the bar, he was assailed by the noise of the patrons, the blare of the pop music and huge cigarette fumes. He peered for a while and saw the man he was looking for. He made his way slowly to the corner table occupied by the man and two other persons he had never met before.

"Welcome to our little party," Edmonds told him, pointing to a chair. Roberts sat down.

"What will you drink?" the Controller-General asked him. "You look as if you need a drink badly."

"Scotch will do," Roberts replied, angry that the solemn-looking leader of the consortium could read his countenance so easily. Edmonds beckoned to a passing waiter and placed Robert's order. The two men continued to stare at the bank president, imprinting all his features into their minds. Roberts was discountenanced by their stares and decided to stay for as short a time as possible.

He gulped the fiery scotch and belched rather loudly. Edmonds waited patiently. "How did it go?" Roberts asked.

"As I told you, the snail has been shelled and ready for shipment. Nicholson will never bother you again."

"About time," Roberts jerked out. "He had me worried and you acted very slowly."

"Slowly but wisely. A decision had to be taken. We work as an organisation. Others had to be contacted. Go home and rest; you have nothing to worry about."

Not long afterwards, Roberts took his leave. Nobody in the stuffy disco hail, except Edmonds and his two associates, noticed that he left without his briefcases; the briefcases that contained all the records of Nicholson's investigations.

"Our friend seems frightened," one of the men said. "He could pose a security problem for us."

"We know that," Edmonds replied. "He is being watched. For now he has been very useful. The time to act will come. Drink up. I have a phone call to make."

Chapter Three

Bogota, Colombia

The mid-day sun beat down on Bogota's main streets. The inevitable character of all overcrowded and rapidly growing cities did not help matters. Vehicles tore in and out of side streets or sped down the choked main streets, with blaring horns. Some drivers cursed at the recklessness of their colleagues. Hawkers shouted their wares and street urchins darted about. Harassed businessmen clutched their briefcases close, to their bodies, scanning the sidewalks for the presence of enterprising pick-pockets.

At a busy intersection, class to the city's squalid Mexican and Indian quarters, a crowd had gathered. A policeman blew his whistle shrilly and the sound of sirens were heard in the distance. Two, men lay in blood pools close to the over-turned wares of a roadside market woman. They were just cut down by a hail of bullets from a rapidly moving Sedan. The crowd surged here and there and the policemen were hard put in. controlling them.

Barely fifty meters from the intersection, towards the palace of the Republic a skimpily dressed prostitute was at war with a patron who had refused to settle his bill. Her sweater had been torn from her shoulders and her mini-skirt was in tatters. The patron fared no better as blood flowed from the deep nail scratches on his face. His shirt was badly torn. The prostitute clung to him desperately squealing in barely audible Spanish.

A group of young Street thugs urged her on, producing sucking sounds with their tips, while their colleagues made quick money picking the pockets and snatching the handbags and wallets of the unwary on lookers. They melted into the gloom of an alley when they saw the shinning helmet of the law.

Inside a bar located on a side street about five hundred meters from the intersection, a serious discussion ensued between two men who had a lot in common. Pablo Rodriquez, the chief prosecutor of Colombia, had every reason to be happy, but that didn't seem to be the case. He stared moodily into space, hardly acknowledging the booming voice of Ricky Tubbs, the American

National Drugs Enforcement operative who helped train and equip the local Colombian Bloque de Basqueda - the force that had tracked down and killed Pablo Escobar in Medellin a few weeks earlier.

Pablo Rodriquez had every reason to be angry. He resented the fact that he bore the same name as the hated and notorious drugs baron and cursed the day he was baptized. He hated too the way his subordinates had been carrying on since Escobar died, as if the war against the drugs trade was over. He knew that the war had hardly started, and that the barons were daily acquiring new tricks.

"Cheer up, old boy," Tubbs, who had called for the celebration, told him. "Can't you take it easy for a while? Our main headache is over. We can pick up the rest whenever we want."

"You think so?" Rodriquez snapped back. "I wouldn't have come had it not been that you wanted this celebration. Escobar may well be dead but our problems remain." He picked up his glass of lemonade and took a sip. Tubbs looked at him, from the corner of his eyes with the expression of a doctor who must be patient with his patient's uninformed babbles.

"I'll give you a lesson in the new drugs trade and the new barons, and you can laugh as much as you wish. For one thing, the entire American and Colombian anti-drugs forces wouldn't have caught up with Escobar had it not been for the support of a faction of the Cali cartel."

"I contradict that, but go on," Tubbs replied.

"You can contradict that to high heavens, but the fact remains that Escobar was betrayed by rival drugs barons; we only stepped in to finish what they started. But that is besides the point. I have lived long enough in Colombia to know its ways.' I studied in your country, Britain and France. I equally know the European and American mind. I read major newspapers, magazines and other publications from four different continents. I keep my eyes and ears open and I listen to people big and small. Most importantly, I am my country's chief prosecutor, so I have virtually unlimited sources of information. I...."

"What are your driving at?" Tubbs cut him short.

"This is supposed to be a celebration over Escobar's death; not the uninteresting details of your life and times." He laughed and reached for his glass of Martini.

"I hate Escobar as much as you do; probably more than you do. I hate the drugs trade and have sworn to fight it till I die; with my life may be. But there is nothing to cheer about. Escobar's death may even be a blessing to the major drugs cartels. He has given them a 1bad name, over-exposed their trade and led agents to know what should otherwise have been hidden."

Rodriquez spoke as if he was never interrupted. He took another sip from his glass and scanned the bar. More than ten of his men were seated like other patrons; nobody knew their identities. They travelled with him everywhere he went. Five more were outside, deployed at obscured areas. Two special unmarked security cars cruised past the bar at ten-minute intervals.

"The drugs trade is acquiring a centralised international character," he resumed. "It has merged with arms-deal, international extortion, blackmail and hired murder. I smell a central organisation somewhere; one that is poised to take over the world."

"Are you sure you are not allowing your imagination run wild?" Tubbs asked. "You need a vacation." He smiled again.

"Listen to me carefully," Rodriquez said tensely. You may laugh today; tomorrow may be different. I'll give you just & little sample. The Cali cartel charts its route from Colombia, Ecuador and Venezuela remains its primary source of production. From there the trade moves to Panama, Guatemala, into Mexico and finally stops at Houston; opens from Colombia to Argentina right up to Italy, France and Amsterdam. Yet, another takes off from Colombia, branches out to Brazil and Paraguay. The Brazilian route moves to Europe through Amsterdam, while the Paraguan route crosses the Mediterranean to the same place. Yet, another passes to Houston through Belize, while a different route laces Lagos, Nigeria, moves through North Africa and stops at Rome, Milan, Naples and other Italian cities. From there the commodity is spread all over Europe."

"Go on," Tubbs whispered, impressed in spite of himself.

"A totally different route," Rodriquez continued, "moves from the Asiatic nations of Thailand and Burma, into Russia, stopping at Moscow and St Petersburg from where it continues, in multiple directions, to Central and Western Europe. Alt these are part of the Burmese-Afghanistan-Iranian-Amsterdam heroin routes; the Afghanistan-Pakistan-Kazakhstan-Moscow-St Petersburg and Western European and the Iranian-Moscow-Ukrainian-Amsterdam, Hashish and raw-opium routes!!"

Rodriguez paused in his monologue 'and peered outside the door. One of the patrol cars flashed past and he nodded. Tubb had abandoned his drinks; he sat bolt upright gazing at Rodriquez respectfully.

"When you recognize that places such as the Islands of Nauru and Vanuatu, and Nassau in the Bahamas, and major cities in Thailand, Hong Kong, Pakistan, United Arab Emirates, Russia, Venezuela, Colombia, Ecuador, Panama, United States and Canada are all drugs-money laundering bases, you will begin to appreciate the scale of this trade, its international scope and the formidable organization that oversees it."

"Phew," Tubbs exclaimed. "This must have taken you a long time to work out. Do you ever do any other thing but chase drugs pushers?" he asked wistfully.

"No other thing. How can I, when I know that even as we speak, millions of drugs-related money is being transferred all over the world via fax, telephone and computer. How can I do any other thing when I am aware that over $1 billion in drugs money is transferred around the major financial centres and capital markets of the world every day. Well, enough of this now. Our celebration is over."

Rodriquez stood up. Tubbs did too. Some of the other patrons in the bar stood in such a manner as not to attract the attention of those around.

"I didn't speak because I love the sound of my voice," Rodiquez said. "I'm passing a message to your government through you. And believe me, many senior members of your government know what

I am talking about." He turned and faced Tubbs when they were close to the door.

"Lest I forget an important thing. There is no way all these things could happen clearly charted and well protected drugs routes, massive movement of drugs across international borders and the transfer of at least, a billion dollars to over fifteen centres in the world every day without a close-knit organisation, a supreme council overseeing it. Mark my words."

As both men stepped out of the door, closely followed by the heavily armed guards inside, a tall, wiry man slid from his back room table and made his way to the beaded curtains that led to the toilets. He entered the male toilet and shut the door after him. He brought out a powerful radio transmitter from his shabby coat pocket, punched some buttons and began speaking rapidly in corrupted Spanish.

Outside the bar, Rodriguez and Tubbs waited patiently for the former's driver to bring out his private car which was parked behind the bar. The two patrol cars had pulled to a stop and their drivers were now idling their engines twenty meters from the bar entrance. People moved busily across the side street, hurrying to their various destinations. Traffic soared past and women paused as they haggled with buyers.

As Rodriguez's car came to a stop in front of the bar, a black and blue coloured goods Van pulled up about five meters away from it. The driver, clad in green overalls, alighted and pushed the side door open. Two other men in green overalls got out from the passenger side of the Van. They too pushed the door open. Three other men emerged from the back of the Van carrying sacks of flour and onions on their shoulders. The driver yelled to the men to get on with their work as he had other deliveries to make. He spoke very loudly, Rodriguez's body-guards relaxed momentarily.

Suddenly, three cats came out of nowhere. Its occupants began spraying bullets everywhere but particularly at the two patrol cars. The Van driver and his four companions dropped down on their knees, sending the goods they were carrying scattered all over. Sub-machine guns emerged from their thick overalls, the opening of which revealed bullet proof vests. They began firing at Rodriquez and Tubbs and the guards standing beside them.

At the first sound of gun shot, Tubb felt a sharp pain on his right shoulder. He fell heavily to the ground, rolled over, flashed out his gun and began to shoot. Rodriguez was not so lucky. The bullets were aimed at his head because his assailants knew that he always wore a bulletproof vest, even to bed. The bullets shattered his skull and he slid to the ground groaning, blood spewing from his mouth. Some of his guards were already hit, but the surviving ones kept their heads and began returning fire. They got three of the men; two in the head and one on the thigh. The surviving three rushed for the cars from which the shooting- had begun. The back-doors were flung open and the men clambered in.

"Go, go, go," the new entrants shouted when they were safely inside. They spoke sharply in Spanish.

Then, the three-cars took the -next turn on the left and sped away.

People began to scream, horrified at the sight of the incident although they were used to the outbreak of violence and painful deaths in Bogota. A police siren wailed in the distance and the surging mass of humanity gave way, nobody could be innocent in the face of the law in the presence of a violent crime.

* * *

Medellin, Colombia

Medellin, a province of sharp contrasts offered a healthy blend of the beautiful and the ugly, the modern and the ancient, and the peaceful and the violent, while its main cities and towns bustled with smartly dressed young men and women who were directly or indirectly involved in the drugs trade and other thriving vices; and while it boasted of sophisticated discotheques comparable to the best in New York, Paris and Amsterdam, its countryside stilt wallowed in complacent traditionalism.

Drugs money had transformed Medellin and this could be seen in the artificiality of its citizens, their loud style of dressing and the exaggerated pace of the life of their local "Yippies. The same could not be said of the remote of the province, the dwelling place of the peasant, most of whom either eked out a subsistent living from the soil or tended the poppy fields of the drugs cartels in conditions less than human.

In one of the shabbier and run-down streets of Medellin's main township, there stood a decrepit hotel that catered for the needs of the none-too-discreet persons fleeing from the law, prostitutes wasted by age, overwork and disease and the numerous flotsam and jetsam of society that still clung to the tail of existence.

That was the site Emmanuelos Dess Animous had made his headquarters under disguise for the past week. A master of the macabre, he calculated that his Medellian enemies would least suspect him in their midst, especially since Escobar had been cut down not quite thirty kilometers away and he was personally held responsible for the betrayal.

He had to be low for a while because the man-hunt for him more by colleagues than from the law was getting more intense. He still had a number of scores to settle with the Medellian cartel but he had to be alive to see that his enemies kiss the dust. He was having a swell time despite the seedy neighbourhood and his ego was more than gratified that he was using Medellin girls as fast as he could in the centre of their province where they least suspected that he would be.

A tall, well-built man in his late thirties who "cut his bone" when he was barely fourteen and had a thin knife scar running down his left cheek, he walked purposely down the city's main thoroughfare clutching a shopping bag in his hand. The scar had been expertly covered; only a very close observation could reveal it, and he avoided close observation as much as he could. His side-burns were fake; so was his thick luxuriant moustache. He walked with a slight limp because of the additional inch added to the right sole of his shoe. His bulkiness was due to the padded clothes he wore because Animous was almost as thin as a bean pole and as deadly as a rattle snake.

He collected his key from the reception clerk, glanced casually at the usual group of men drinking in the lobby and made his way to his room along a foul-smelling hall-way.

He stabbed his key into the key hole and opened his door, which he locked when he was safely inside. The young girl on the bed looked up at him admiringly and purred sweetly.

"You are early today, daddy," she said. "Yes, my dear. Come and give daddy a..."

She slid off the bed and the bedding fell away from her. Naked and fresh, she padded across the threadbare carpet and got to him. She slipped her hands across his neck and gave him a long, warm, passionate kiss.

"I'm ready for daddy whenever he is ready," she murmured and walked back to the bed, rolling her hips suggestively as she went.

Aminous stripped off his padded jackets and trousers, and, having only his pants and singlet on, walked to the door and carefully placed his gun on the occasional side table with the safety catch off. He learnt that it was always better to shoot first and ask questions later.

He lay beside 'the girl, a sixteen year old he -had 'met on the streets a couple of days earlier, who had survived his vicious temper and strange ways for over three days now; a feat none of his other girls had quite attained. Her name was Anita, and she was in the bloom of her youth.

He began to fondle her breasts and thighs. She purred softly-and clung to him. Her excited cries aroused him and he began to breathe heavily. As he rose slightly to enter her, a sharp knock came on the door. It was the waiter who had- a special present from the manager for him for having stayed so long with them and paid his rent on time too.

He hesitated in his motion and thought for a white. What the hell, he reasoned. Better to get rid of the bugger and back to his pleasurable business. He slid on his shorts, picked up his gun which he shoved behind his back waist band. He gave sign to Anita to cover herself up and she pulled the bed clothes right up to her chin. He peered through the keyhole and saw the waiter with an ice bucket containing the hotel's special offer, a red wine and fruits. He opened the door and beckoned to the smiling waiter. As the waiter stepped into the room, two shadowy figures stepped out of an alcove in the side walls and converged on him.

"Make no stupid moves, Aminous," they said. "No stupid moves," they ordered in Spanish. They each had an automatic sub-machine gun pointed at his stomach and head. They pushed him back into the room and closed the door after them. They gave a sign to the waiter who hurried out of the room and began running down the corridor.

"The consortium sends its love," one of the men told him, as he reached out and snatched the gun from Animous' waist band. "We know who you are; have always known your audacity and foolish courage. You have been watched day and night. Your hour of reckoning has come.

The other man kept Anita covered, threatening her with his silencer gun lest she screamed. Animous watched them apprehensively. He knew that they were professionals like himself and would make a good job of their business. Better to get them talking while he found a way out of the jam he was in.

"You are mistaken, good brothers. I'm not the man you seek. I am just a peasant from the village who wants to enjoy a bit of the good life in the city. Many elders in my village can testify for me. I can take you to them."

"No need for that," the first who spoke said again. "No need for that." We have heard all we wanted to hear. "Escobar will go to heaven, but your soul will dwell with the devil himself."

He raised his gun and pointed it at Animous' forehead. The latter bounced himself to spring'. The dull echo of the silencer gun reverberated dimly in the shabby room. Animous was already lounging for his assailant, his hands out-stretched, a snarling expression in his eyes and mouth. The bullet caught him high on the forehead. Another through his mouth and throat. The third pierced his heart. The impact threw him backwards and he fell on the floor, taking the occasional table with him. His fall shook the thin floor.

As Anita started a shrill scream, rapid shots thudded into her body which began to shake and quiver. Blood spurted all over the sheet and her convulsing hands pushed the sheets away to reveal her milky white breasts and creamy thigh.

The two surveyed the scene, and, satisfied with their work, made their way silently out of the desolate room. Once in the corridor, one of them - the one who spoke earlier - said: "Report to the local council immediately. I will place an urgent call to the consortium as soon as I get back into town." Then they vanished as quietly and as stealthily as they had come.

Chapter Four

The CIA Director, Chris Williams, looked up from his desk and regarded the DEA chief, Peterson, doubtfully. He inclined his head and squinted at his visitor from a corner of his eyes. His gaze spoke volumes, for he was undeniably unmoved by the latter's briefing. How was he to accept that an international organisation was involved in the production and distribution of hard drugs, and in money laundering? And that probably, the same organisation had infiltrated the illegal arms trade, not essentially for its commercial interest, but for some other dubious military and political objectives?

He removed his horn-rimmed spectacles and placed it on the desk. Then, he brought out a plain white handkerchief and proceeded to wipe his face. Williams reflected that Peterson had spoken persuasively for about fifteen minutes and seemed to know what he was talking about, but some of the facts he revealed were so mind-boggling that he refused to accept them. He wondered whether his refusal was based on any objective premise or that he was reluctant, if not unwilling, to admit that the other man had information which by virtue of his position, lie ought to have had too.

Peterson remained still and watched the CIA boss speculatively. He knew that he should have waited for at least one more month before confronting the CIA chief with his information - a period during which he would have done some further digging. But something kept on telling him that there was no time to lose; that the opposition was getting ready to strike.

"Look, Peterson," Williams said. "I know how you feel, but the' information you have is not something I can pass on to the State Department, not to talk of the White House."

Williams relaxed visibly. He was beginning to doubt his own intelligence network. He was no ordinary political appointee but a seasoned career intelligence officer who had worked his way to the top, paid his dues and was a beneficiary of the president's policy of professionalising the various agencies of government. It would have been an embarrassing situation were he to report Peterson's findings when he had nothing himself to offer from the activities of his own men.

Of course, he could appropriate Peterson's ideas as his but that could come unstuck anytime for the wily DEA chief had sufficient pull in Washington to get his story heard without going through the CIA. So, the best option was to lead the man away from such a dangerous territory as this, persuade him to see that he had allowed his imagination to run wild, give himself enough time and then mount a more effective strategy of substantiating such claims.

Peterson was fully aware of the workings of Williams' mind and smiled wryly to himself. He had backed away hastily- from -his original position because he did not want to make an enemy of the CIA boss. Had Williams been an ordinary political appointee, it would have been different. In that case, he would be dealing with any of the deputy directors who were professional men as himself. That would have strengthened his hand. But to embarrass a career officer who was clearly losing his grip over intelligence details may have jeopardized his career.

"But Sir," he began, "I still think that you should call a meeting of the top operatives covering the South American, European, French and Offshore Zones and alert them of this emerging scenario."

"Sure" Williams replied. "Leave that to .me; I'll handle it."

"And one more thing," Peterson added. Williams pricked his ears at this last request.

"One more thing," Peterson repeated, as if he was not sure of the answer he would receive. "I suggest that you arrange for Ricky Tubbs to be flown back immediately from Bogota. You may wish to interview him yourself. My man just came back from Bogota a few days ago, and I want to assume that though he gave me some of the brief which came from Tubbs, he would keep his mouth shut."

Williams seemed to have hesitated. "What kind of attention is he receiving in Colombia?" he asked.

"He is in one of their best hospitals and is guarded day and night. I think that he wasn't the target of the attack and that the decision to eliminate Rodriquez was taken long before their meeting. Yet, you can't put anything beyond these bastards. The entire Colombian security force is riddled with corruption and careerism. Some of the key officers are in the payroll of the drugs barons. Tubbs may be sold away for all we know. Those chaps are afraid of their own shadows and they may be wondering what Rodriquez might have told Tubbs."

"Okay, leave the arrangements to me. I'll have him flown back immediately. I'll use one of our special jets. I'll let you know the moment he is back and where he is."

"Thank you, Sir," Peterson said, very much relieved. He got up from his chair, picking up the file folder in front of him. He made his way to the door and shut it carefully when he stepped out into the outer office.

Williams remained brooding over his desk some minutes after Peterson had gone. His back hunched and his mind busy, he thought about the next line of action. Then, having made up his mind, he picked up the intercom and spoke gently to his secretary.

"Tell Simons that I want to see him today as soon as possible; not earlier than 4 p.m." He dropped the receiver back on its cradle and glanced at his wrist watch. The time was 2.05 p.m. Time enough for him to do a little paper work and still meet with the Under-Secretary of State for Asian affairs over the latest developments in Kampuchea and North Korea before his all-important talk with his Deputy Director in charge of South America and the Caribbeans. He reached for a file and began studying some documents.

* * *

Simons picked up the telephone receiver on the third ring. He pressed some buttons and the call was instantly unscrambled. It was the night after his meeting with Williams. He was stretched out on the sofa in his second sitting-room, a highball in his hand, when the telephone rang. He usually unscrambled most of his calls. One stayed healthy and alive that way.

"Yes," he whispered into the receiver.

"How did it go; I mean the meeting today with Williams?" The voice at the other end was unmistakable. Simons lost some of the colour in his face. He held the receiver tightly.

"It wasn't good; not good at all."

"What was it all about?"

"We need a meeting to talk things over. It may be unsafe to discuss such matters over the telephone," he said quickly.

"It's as safe as it could be. What did you discuss with Williams?" the voice repeated.

Simons sweated slightly.

"The DEA chief briefed him about the possibility of your existence," he said. "Mind you," he said hastily, "just mere speculation; no hard facts."

"Shelve your opinion for the moment. Just go on."

'There must be a leak somewhere," Simons opined. "Somebody must have talked. They have sketchy details about the latest arms shipment."

"Just keep me briefed," the voice snapped.

"There is one other thing," Simons added "The American agent who was with Rodriguez when he was murdered will be brought back to the USA very soon. He's prepared to sing his head off."

There was a pause at the other end of the line. When the voice came back, it seemed to be floating from far away.

"Let me know when he is due back; the time and the place. Thanks." There was a click and the connection was broken.

Jack Edmonds regarded the four men who were with him.

"Gentlemen," he said, "there is an assignment that must be taken care of before long."

At his own end, Simons gripped the receiver and then returned it slowly. He got up and 'freshened his high-ball. "Thanks," the Controller-General had said. He rarely complimented anyone. Simone regarded his living-room and smiled to himself. Fears forgotten, and basking in the euphoria of being regarded highly, he began to do sums in his head about his huge financial rewards placed discreetly in an offshore accounts.

***

The light jet circled over the clear sky and began a leisurely descent. There were four me aboard it. The pilot and the co-pilot who doubled as the flight engineer, an air hostess who was a DEA staff and Ricky Tubbs still groggy and Covered in bandage. There was a small clearing and a long stretch of road that served as the runway. For off to the right was a shabby, nondescript house that served as the operational base of the DEA patrol team. The house, the clearing and the runway had not been in use for a long time.

It was the appropriate choice made by the CIA when it decided to extradite Tubbs back to the USA. Only the CIA Director, the DEA Director and a handful of core staffers on both sides knew of the plan: An advance team of three special agents had been sent to monitor the site; the real welcoming party would arrive about ten minutes after touch down. The advance party knew nothing of this arrangement.

The light jet roared along the runway, dispelling a column of dust behind it. It came to a bumpy stop and began its steady droning. The door was yanked open and an won ladder lowered to the ground. The three special agents came out of the shabby house and made their way casually to the plant. Then above the roar of the aircraft engines, the men heard the subdued noise of a car racing to the compound. They thought little of it; suspecting that it was the get-away car.

A car and a bus, each bearing the OEA markings, came to a standstill in front of the house. Seven men jumped out of them, three of them wearing DEA uniforms. As the three men and the hostess made their way towards the three agents, one of the men who alighted from he bus brought out a hand grenade from his coat pocket and, lying flat on the scrubby ground threw it high into their midst. His colleagues laid on the ground too and opened up with automatic weapons they had at the ready. The noise of ricocheting bullets filled the atmosphere. Caught unprepared, the men staggered here and there, screaming. The air hostess dashed back to the jet and lay behind its back tyres. Tubbs caught the first blast flush on the forehead. He dropped to the ground. When the carnage was over three men dashed towards the plane and balled the screaming and trashing hostess from where she was hiding.

They dragged her to the car. One of them aimed a shot at the fuel tank of the jet and from a distance fired a smoke bomb inside it. He jumped inside the car with the rest and the two vehicles tore out of the compound.

One of the DEA agents who was only wounded brought out his trans-receiver and began dialing frantically. He was still calling headquarters three minutes later when the Special DEA team that came to take Tubbs to his new hospital raced into the premises in a four-wheel drive. They jumped out of the trooper and forced their way through the thick smoke of the burning plane to where their dead and wounded comrades lay.

Chapter Five

It had been raining steadily for a couple of hours. Rain and the gentle drift of snow flakes. The streets of Washington DC glistened as the snowflakes got crushed by passing vehicles to form a thin flow of water. The curbs too were shiny, except in places where the gravel had become uneven from wear.

People drifted by in large overcoats, mackintoshes and umbrellas. Traffic was as thick as ever and the mood everywhere was one of expectancy tinged with a measure of foreboding. It was late winter. A particularly troublesome period that heralded the welcome spring.

Trouble was not only to be felt in the streets of Washington DC. It was deep-seated in the sheltered offices of the White House. The president of the United States of America was at conference with his close security aides. Their mood reflected the mood in the streets; great expectation mixed with a certain fear of the unknown. With him were the Secretary of State, Y.W. Richards; the CIA Director, Williams; the Director of the DEA, Peterson; and his Chief National Security Adviser, Henry Jerome.

"Gentlemen," the president began, shifting slightly in his' swivel chair, "You are all welcome. May we begin as I have another engagement in an hour's time."

Williams did not need any further invitation. It had been agreed among them that he should do "the presentation, being senior to the DEA Director, and as the other staffers were all working directly for the president. The briefing was as much for the president as it was for them.

"Mr President," he began, "there are certain information that we have which points to the fact that the international trade in narcotics is assuming a very dangerous dimension which may pose a threat to the survival of our democracy." He chose his words carefully. He never looked down for once at the sheaf of papers in front of him. He was well prepared.

"There were a series of apparently unconnected events," he continued, "that point towards the existence of a centralised monopoly that oversees the trade in hard drugs. I will quickly enumerate them. One was the brutal murder of Nicholson, the vice-president of First American Bank Shares. The murder was apparently without motive as a robbery was recorded at the scene of the incident. Yet, further investigations by the police revealed that he had in his apartment, scraps of d9cuments that suggested that he was carrying out a major investigation about the involvement of his bank in drug money laundering. The second incident was the equally brutal murder of Pablo Rodriquez, the Colombian chief prosecutor. He was with Ricky Tubbs, a special DEA agent who helped train the local force that eliminated Pablo Escobar. Tubbs was also murdered a few days ago by hit men that impersonated DEA agents."

"Where did this last incident take place?" the Secretary of State asked.

"In a lonely and partly disused DEA post in New Mexico," Williams replied. "He was being flown in for debriefing."

"In the past six weeks," he continued, "there has been an upsurge in the illegal arms trade and most of the transactions were carried out by third parties who apparently never knew about the final destination of the arms they purchased. On the surface, most of these incidents are unrelated. But our men have been working on them. The report we have now is far more unifying than when we started." He paused and turned even a few of the sheets in front of him. The other persons waited patiently for him to continue.

"For a start," he finally said, "three of the shells of the bullets that killed Nicholson, Rodriquez and Tubbs are identical and were fired from the same chambers. That established the fact that at least, one or two people were involved- in the killing of the three men. Another interesting fact that emerged is that two for the men who were shot dead during the attack on Rodriquez and Tubbs were involved in six of the illegal arms purchases and in the murder of Animous, a small-time drugs pusher who helped track down Escobar.

Finally, our preliminary investigations also revealed that most of the arms purchases were undertaken by a non-existent body, legally speaking, which nevertheless operates in about nine South American, European and Asian countries. What this means is that the over $100m worth of arms sold in the past six weeks were bought by an illegal agency whose shareholders and directors are, for all intents and purposes, non-existent."

Williams paused again and was rewarded by the worried look on the face of the president, the avid interest in the eyes of the Secretary of State and the frightened countenance of the National Security Adviser. He never was one to make a fool of himself and though he was well aware that what he knew or thought he knew could jeopardize the lives of many of his own operatives. Williams was immensely satisfied that he was getting the attention he wanted. "When we add up these facts," he continued, "the fact that the same people killed three different men in three different locations at separate times; that some of those involved in the killings were linked up in major arms purchases by a single organisation, as shadowy as it may be, and that Nicholson's death may have been a drug hit, we were forced to conclude that a syndicate has been established to co-ordinate and expand the international drugs trade. This expansion involves the purchase of enough arms to topple about twenty small South American, Asian, Middle East and African countries."

"What can you make out of all this?" the president asked his national security adviser, still looking worried.

Henry Jerome was a veteran intelligence officer who managed to combine his legendary professionalism with an astute political ambition. He was simply good for the job and the president relied heavily on him in state security and intelligence matters.

He cleared his throat and spoke slowly. "On the face of it, the facts presented indicate strongly that a global network has been established by the major drug cartels, and that their primary objective now may well be the combination of financial reward with enormous political and military clout. Nevertheless, we cannot jump to any conclusions. First, the existence of this international body has to be objectively ascertained. Second, the recent illegal arms deals must be thoroughly scrutinised. Finally, I suggest that we move carefully in order not to tie our hands before we have the necessary corroborating details. I suggest that a liaison officer be appointed between the CIA, the DEA and the White House who will co-ordinate the investigations and act as a bridge between the various anti-drug agencies."

The President smiled for the first time since the briefing commenced. He nodded towards the Secretary of State. "I go along with Henry. There is nothing we can achieve unless the steps he enumerated are taken.

"Do you have a candidate for this important job?" the President asked the CIA Director.

Without hesitation, Williams responded. "With your permission, I suggest that Michael Simons-be given the job. He has been on the job for over twenty years. He has worked in the DEA and the Special Forces. He has also had a stint as .a White House intelligence officer. His area of specialisation is the South American and Caribbean countries - the major drug zones of the world."

The President nodded slowly. The DEA director was equally satisfied.

"Get your man briefed as soon as possible," the president said. "Let him raise a special team from all the available agencies. While he will be giving you periodic briefings, he should report directly to the office of the National Security Adviser. The meeting is closed."

The men filed out slowly, satisfied that the day was not wasted, and sure that the bleak Washington DC morning held more of a promise than a frightening foreboding.

* * *

Festac Town. Lagos, Nigeria

The mid-day tropical sun blazed on the paved and tree-lined streets of Festac Town's 26th Avenue. The area was previously a dense mangrove swamp which money had now transformed. Strikingly beautiful houses abounded in the Avenue. There seemed to be a silent competition going on between the owners and developers of the properties. Satellite dishes gleamed atop the roofs of the houses and the streets were nearly choked with sleek luxury cars. Various car brands jostled for position on the dirt-free streets. The area was not called "commodity" Avenue for nothing.

In one of the posh houses well off the main street. a meeting was in progress. The host, a tall, bulky man in his mid-thirties was busy supervising the drinks. Known simply as America he radiated confidence and exuded opulence. Seated on the sofas were his close associates. Lord Micky, Angelus and Tubby Boy complimented one another, flashing their diamond bracelets; rings and designer attires. A rather silent man sat slightly away from the rest. He occasionally glanced at a group of young girls who sat in the second sitting room (separated from the. first by a mahogany cabinet), discussing animatedly. He licked his lips occasionally and his eyes had a fierce sparkle.

America walked over to him and whispered something in his ears. He then stood up and clapped his hands. One of the girls came over laughing. She wore a thin blouse that barely concealed her breasts and her mini-skirt hardly covered her crotch. "Take care of our friends," America ordered her. "Show him how hospitable we can be." She stretched out her hand and the silent man gripped it. Then they both made their way out of the living room to the admiring cackles of the party.

"Our friend is tired," America told the other three.

"He deserves a rest. Now back to business," he added, going over to a single sofa and lowering his huge frame into it.

"You are all aware how disorganised our trade has become," he said. "We have done a lot since our last deliberation, and since Tobby Boy came back from Jo'burg. Now, a new message has been delivered through our friend from America, who has just left. We are told to keep the outfit the way it is now; not to expand and not to break fresh grounds."

"Why?" several voices asked.

"Easy, easy," America implored them. "The instruction 'is that a five-man committee will soon be visiting and that it is better for them to see a real structure on the ground, rather than a large, disunited group of individual competitors."

"I go along with you," Angelus intoned.

America glanced at the other three. They nodded.

"Our friend will be going back in two days' time, so we have enough time to come up with our proposals and objections. Africa is our orbit and nobody can deny us the opportunity to be fully integrated into the main stream. But that can wait for now. These lovely girls are becoming very lonely and must be wondering whether we've still got it."

He leered at his partners who grinned and started rising from their seats. "Solving their problems is our preoccupation," America added. "The other business can wait till later."

They moved as a group towards the waiting girls who had already adopted seductive postures when they knew the time for action was at hand.

Chapter Six

The jeep drew very close to the customs check, its headlamps piercing through the thick darkness. There were four men in the jeep, including the driver. One of them was smoking a long brown cigar. The lights spotted a steel bar that was thrown across the road, and held on either side by huge rods. Beyond the steel bar was the tiny customs shed, a makeshift affair of old brick and corrugated iron sheets.

The jeep drew to a halt. Three men came out of the shed and walked indifferently to the jeep. They were dressed in brown khaki uniforms and leather boots. Each had arm assault rifle slung over his shoulder. A man got out of the jeep and walked towards the customs patrol team1 a sheet of paper in his left hand. He wore a three-piece suit under an overcoat. He wore a hat, the trim of which was well pulled down to his brow.

When he got close to the patrol team, he jerked his hat back and greeted them in Spanish. He extended the papers and paused to light another cigar. The men studied the papers closely and one of them handed them back to him. The other two shook their heads and motioned to the man to get into the jeep and drive away. He began to argue with them, his voice rising steadily till it violated the silence of the border area.

A ship hooted in the distance, and the light from a distant lighthouse could be seen over the immense expanse of the sea that lay beyond the border post.

The argument attracted the attention of another man in the customs shed who came out wiping his hands on the seat of his khaki trousers. His face broke into a broad grin when he saw the man in the overcoat. His three companions relaxed and made way for him.

"Welcome friend Guttfried," he said in Spanish "long time no see." They shook hands.

"I was beginning to wonder what was amiss," the man who was addressed as Guttfried replied. "I thought that we had sealed all the arrangements."

"Indeed, we have," the man said. "Pardon the zeal of my men. Such an embarrassment will never occur again." He was a short, thick-set man with closely cropped, thinning hair on his large dome. He whispered something to his colleagues who now grinned at Guttfried and shook hands with him warmly.

One of them went to the steel bar and raised it as Guttfried walked with the thick-set man, whose name was Espado Yortega, into the customs shed. They were there for about five minutes. Guttfried walked back to the jeep, entered and slammed the door. The jeep drove off into the darkness, and the driver could still see the waving shadowy outline of the four men.

An immense forest surrounded the dirt road on either side and the branches of the trees hung very close to the road. Then without warning, the forest disappeared and a large expanse of water emerged. The jeep bumped over the sandy road and came to a stop in front of a shabby rundown building. Its doors swung open and the four men came down. The door of the Mariner's house opened and two men came towards them. One had a sweatshirt over his greasy jeans and canvass shoes. The other was shirtless and his hairy chest was revealed by the dull lights from the several ships that lay docked at the harbour.

"You are dead on time, Mr. Guttfried," the man in the sweatshirt said. "Dead on time. The shipment came just over twenty minutes ago."

Guttfried grunted but said nothing. The two men turned on their heels and the rest followed them. They passed several sailors walking about the empty spaces. Smoke mists came from one of the houses farther down the dockyard and the hoarse cries of drunken men were transmitted by the fair wind to their ears.

They came to the railing on the gang plank and slowed their pace. The water lapped gently beneath their feet, rocking their gang plank slowly. A ship was berthed a short way from the gang plank. They passed through a jetty and gained entry to the ship. The Captain, a burly man in his mid-fifties, was waiting on the top staircase. He shook hands with the men and led them to the upper deck.

They came to a narrow passage that was dimly lit by naked bulbs. At the end of the passage was a steel door. It was securely locked. The Captain opened the steel door and pushed it back with great effort. A goodly sized container, covered with brown tarpaulin was in the large room. The Captain and the two dockers 'pulled the tarpaulin away and began to unhinge the iron bars that secured the mouth of the container.

Guttfried and his three companions watched 'the whole activity with detached interest. The wooden panel was forced back arid the inside was revealed. Hundreds of crates were packed inside the container. The Captain climbed into the container through a side stair-case and beckoned to Guttfried to join him.

He forced one of the crates open with the aid of a steel crossbar that lay on the floor of the container. Inside the crate were components of sub-machine guns. Guttfried peered closely and touched the oily metals. Another case was opened which contained parts of grenade launchers. Guttfried nodded again.

"The shipment is complete," the Captain said. "The papers are in my office. One of my men will deliver them with' you in that way you will now that I'm a man of my word." He led the way back to his office to complete this dangerous and hazardous transaction.

Back in the shabby Mariner's' house. Guttfried brought out a mobile telephone. He dialed some numbers and pressed the handsetto his ear. "Jack, it's me," Guttfried replied. "The birds have come home to roost. The shipment of the Olives went without a hitch. Arrange for their delivery in a week's time.

Salute Marseilles for me." He pressed some more buttons and dropped the handset back in his overcoat pocket.

"Julius," he called one of the men he came with. "Stay with these chaps till the whole transaction is over. I'm informed the truck is already waiting. The Customs men will give you no problem. I'm relying on you." The man he called Julius nodded and went back to the gin he had abandoned on a ramshackle table.

Guttfried Von Guttingberg went outside the room with the remaining two men climbed into the jeep. The others came outside the broken- down door and watched. The jeep roared into the night sending a shower of sandy soil on both sides.

* * *

The mountain breeze lapped on the sides of the lodge deep in the French Alps. The woods creaked and the soft rustling sound of birch leaves on the wooden roof was very audible. Below in the valley, the sea lapped gently on the shoreline. Occasionally, waves rose and fell with the movement of the sea breeze.

The guest lodge was situated in a lonely part of the Alps, with only a single access road that wound itself around the mountain. It was totally covered by tall elm and birch trees, except for the narrow track that led to its frontage and the tiny clearing that lay directly in front of the door.

It was shortly before dawn and the hillside was already showing signs of the approaching day. Tiny streaks of light penetrated the dense forest overhead and threw blurred shadowy patterns on the leaf-strewn ground. The lodge was silent save for the patter of the feet of the two armed guards and the noise by the cook/steward in the outhouse a short distance away from the lodge.

Jean Jacques D'Atmand, the French Minister for Internal Affairs and National Security, raised his head from the pillow and reached for his illuminated watch on the table just over his head. The time was 5.06 a.m. He lay back with a satisfied grunt but kept his eyes open. The woman by his side purred in her half-sleep and reached for his neck. Their mouths found each other's and for a moment, they were caught in the passionate magic of the moment. The bedding rolled away to reveal the well-tanned long, tapering legs of his companion. Their breathing came in short jerks and for a while there was another sound in the room.

Then D'Atmand gave a start and sprang out of bed gathering his sleeping robe around him. He made his way bare-footed to another door that led off the bedrooms to the toilet. The woman on the bed heard the sound of running water and relaxed further back on the soft sheets.

"What's the hurry darling?" she called out when D'Atmand came back into the room. It's not daylight yet, is it? And I thought we still have two days to ourselves. D'Atmand grinned at her. "I

41

thought so too myself till last night. Something came up and I have to be in Paris before noon."

"Something that could interrupt your well-earned vacation? Come on Jean, you don't have to kill yourself with work. Your deputy can handle that."

D'Atmand was already dressing up. He sat on the side of the bed to put on his shoes. The woman half-rose on her elbow, her arms circling his neck. Her breasts were exposed.

"Not this particular business," he replied to her last question.

"There are certain matters that only a minister can attend to, and this happens to be one of them." She made effort at sulking and dropped back on the bed with feigned resignation.

"Come on, honey," she said appealingly. "There will be other times. The jeep will take you back to town. I will contact you in a week's time. After you've had your stuffy little meeting about Street robbers in Paris."

"No need to be sarcastic. This is an important state business. Important European business, for that matter. It's a meeting of EEC National Security Ministers and the subject is the new drugs threat, if you must know."

"Drugs?" she asked. "What has drugs got to do with your job?"

"Plenty baby, plenty," and he grinned at her, patting her flank.

"Word came out of Washington that a new drugs cartel may have been formed and that its mischief may even extend to political exploitations in Europe and elsewhere. We have to devise a means to stop them."

"Wow, you and your petty state business," she said. "Of course, I'm not interested. It's only you I want." Her face was blank as she said this.

"I know you are not; that is why 1 had to explain to you." He bent down and kissed her full, moist ups. '1 will be back in ten minutes' time. Lat me give instructions to my chaps."

He left the room silently. Barbara Alumineza listened to the sound of his foot-steps till they died away. Then she sprang out of bed quickly, throwing the bed clothes away. Quite naked, she pressed on a hidden knob. Another recess opened and she brought out a very tiny disk with an adhesive gum on the reverse side. She glanced over her shoulder and pattered to the door end locked it. She reached for D'Atmand's personal briefcase - the particular one that he went everywhere with and began turning the opening dial she had long mastered. The case sprang open. She stuck the tiny disc - a powerful mini-recorder that was the pride of the espionage industry - in an obscure part of the case and snapped it shut. She dialed again, till she had set the numbers to the positions she had found them.

Quickly, she went to the door, unlocked it and lay down on the bed.

Jack Edmonds must know about this, she thought. Must know about it, even before the next rendezvous with D'Atmand when she would retrieve the disc and send it to the Consortium. Thoroughly relaxed, she waited for the return of the minister.

The two men met at a particular busy street in downtown Rio de-Janeiro. The crowd bustled past them. Hawkers shouted their wares. The traffic was as tick and noisy as ever. They hardly glanced at each other when they met from the opposite direction. Yet they held out their hands and took the direction from where one of them came. They walked for a short distance. Things are happening," Jack Edmonds said. "First, the news about Simons. Then Guttfried's successful arms deal. Barbara has a lot to say but you know her. She takes here times. Arrange a meeting of the select commit without delay. We will meet in UAE. Let the Sheiks play hosts for once." He spoke without pause, hardly glancing at his companion.

"Right away," Caesar Leopoldo Oscar said. "Consider it done." He sometimes doubled as the Secretary of the Consortium, a particularly dignified title for the son of a Colombian peasant who had done well for himself. They came to the entrance of a gaudy, neon-plastered bar and hesitated as tourists were wont to do. Then, shrugging their shoulders they pushed the swing doors open and entered the stuffy bar.

Chapter Seven

They had the house well surrounded. There were three of them; Wong Wanci, of the Thai special anti-drugs forces, Thu Chang of the same bureau and Joe Lucas, a special agent of the DEA on loan to the Thai authorities. Their informant, a repentant drugs dealer, lay in the shadows a couple of meters away from where the men crouched. Dusk was falling rapidly but the noise of Central Bangkok was as ferocious and intense as ever.

Lights blazed from various neon signs, and from the numerous bars, night clubs, restaurants and residential homes that gave Bangkok its distinct character. Cars jostled for prominence on the road while the sidewalk was taken over by the countless number of people who moved about like columns of ants.

The house the men were watching lay a short distance away from the main street. Most of the floors were in darkness but the sixth and seventh floors had lights showing through of the windows. The men were sure that the shipment of cocaine had taken place; the informant had made sure of that. They were sure too that the drugs had been packed in small plastic bags ready for the exchange that they knew would take place that same night.

They had toyed with the idea of confronting the barons and couriers during the exchange; that would mean killing a number of birds with one stone, but they were not certain where the exchange would take place. The informant had not gotten adequate information on that. So their best bet was to burst the operation before the exchange did take place.

Joe Lucas looked at his watch. The time was 6.23 p.m. They had been waiting for over forty minutes now and knew that their waiting was not over yet. Their two special patrol cars with the back-up team were parked about fifty meters down the relatively quiet street, well away from the busy main thoroughfare.

They were well covered by the tall plants that covered the vacant lot next to the building they were watching. Joe Lucas was about to whisper something to one of the men when his sharp eyes picked up the headlights of a fast approaching car. He slid back into the bush, lay flat on the ground and waited. The long car came down fast and stopped in front of the building, with a screech of tortured tyres. Three men tumbled out of it, each dressed in loud ill-fitting suits. They walked rapidly to the building and were soon out of sight. Another man - probably the driver came out of the car after a few minutes and leant against it. After a short while, he lit a cigarette and began to puff contentedly.

About fifteen minutes passed. Joe Lucas half-stood up and gave a sign to his colleagues. He began to creep towards the parked car making as little noise as possible. When he was a couple of meters away from the car, the driver paused in his smoking, threw the stub down and cocked his ears. Joe lay very still, watching the man's moves closely. After a while, the man gays up his tensed posture and leant on the car. He brought out something which he unwrapped. Joe began his dangerous moves again. He could see the man clearly now. He was a thin, wiry creature with a pock-marked face and thinning hair. He wore a windcheater over corduroy trousers. Joe's hands closed over a large stone. He flung it away from himself very fast, dropping flat on the ground as he did. The man swung around, his hand in the pocket of his windcheater.

Now Joe whispered, coiled himself and sprang on the man. Shod, and the momentum of his assault carried the man over and knocked him to the ground Joe's hands reached for the man's neck and tightened around it brutally. The man thrashed for a while and lay still. Joe stood up, dusted himself over and gave a sharp piercing whistle. He ran lightly to the left of the building, watching the progress of the two agents from the corner of his eyes. Wong made his way to the right, while Chang made a detour and circled the building from the back.

Joe reached for a stack pipe and hung on to it. He reached up and pushed up a closed catch-window. He jerked himself, got a footing appeared inside a dark room through the open window. They had rehearsed their entry very well. They knew that the men were on the sixth floor, the upper floor being occupied by an Estate agent.

He flashed his light and turned the door handle. The door

opened inwards without a sound. Close to it was the staircase. He made his way silently to it, looking constantly up as he wept.

Chang had discovered the fire escape route which he pulled down. It creaked softly and came to a halt near his feet. Without wasting time he ran up it lightly and was soon on the sixth floor landing. He tried the door that faced him and it opened outwards. He entered a disused kitchen/store room, opened its unlocked door and gained entry to a dark corridor. He lay crouched on the side of the wall and waited.

Wong has a stout rope with spiked hooks fixed to one end. He twirled the rope very fast in the air and flung it up calculatedly. It hit the space between the railings on the fifth floor. He pulled it hard till sweat broke out on his face. The hold was solid. He wiped his gloved hands on the seat of his trousers, gripped the rope and began to climb. When he pulled his legs over the railing, he removed the hooks from their grip, coiled the rope and put it back inside the duff le bag he carried across his shoulder. He reached up and opened the window above his head, got a grip on the wooden frame and heaved himself up.

* * *

The room was rectangular in shape and quite long. A long table dominated its centre. On top of it were two sacks of refined cocaine. Smaller plastic bags lay scattered on the table. Four men sat round the table scooping the white powder into the bags. The room was very hot, its windows being securely closed. The men were sweating. Three men paced around the room, the same men that came in the long car. A guard stood just before the door, his assault rifle held in readiness. He was alert.

Joe Lucas crawled just behind the door. Wong stood in the shadows a few meters from him, his gun held at the ready. Chang lay behind Joe giving him cover with his gun. There was a space of about two inches between the door and the floor and a bright light showed through it. Joe crept close to the door, put his head on the floor and looked into the room. He could identify the feet of the guard.

They had decided that shock tactics was the best method to

carry out this operation and they had rehearsed their procedures having cased the joint a number of times. Joe dropped on his knees, pushed his submachine gun out and squeezed the trigger rapidly. The sound of splinting wood and a yell came with the roar of the gunfire. The door sagged. He came up with a flying kick and the door tore off its hinges. He tumbled into the room with Wong, rolled over and crouched on the floor, his gun still at the ready. Chang opened fire down the corridor aiming high at the window in front of him. The wood shattered under the impact of the assault. He rushed into the room, landing with a jarring thud. He too rolled over and came up on his knees, his rifle held over his shoulder.

The guard lay curled up near where Joe crouched, blood oozing out of his chest and trickling out of his mouth. He was quite dead. The men working on the table had all stood up, with their hands held over their heads. One of the three pacing men had reached for his gun the moment the first crash came. He fired rapidly towards the door. There was counter firing from Wong and he dropped his gun, clutched his stomach and fell on his knees.

The three agents stood up slowly, watching the men intently.

"Special Squad!" "Stay where you are," Joe shouted.

The sound of a siren tore through the hot night and a moment later, the sound of pounding feet was heard on the staircase. A few minutes later, the back-up team entered the room with guns and handcuffs.

* * *

The persistent knock on the door woke Joe from sleep with a muted curse. The girl who lay by his side said something in her sleep, rolled over and curled up again. Joe went to the door and peered through the door hole. His breathing stopped. Standing there was the First Secretary of the American Embassy and another embassy official he had met a couple of times.

"Just a moment," he called out. He shook the girl wake and dragged her to the bathroom, making signs to her not to make a noise. He collected here clothes and other belongings and dropped them in the bathroom. He closed the bathroom door behind him and then unlatched the chain that held the door.

The two men steeped in, apologising for their unannounced visit. The time was 6.03 a.m. Joe had barely had four hours sleep because, he only managed to get out of Thai anti-drugs headquarters a few minutes before 2 a.m.

The First Secretary brought out a couple of documents from his briefcase which he laid on the table.

"Your job in Thailand is over for now," he matter-of-factly.

"Here's your ticket back to Washington. Here's your new travelling papers. And here's your letter of commendation from the Thai Government. Report to Mr Simons of the CIA head office. You are specifically requested to see him before meeting with the head of the desk of South East Asia operations. Any questions?"

Joe shook his head, collecting all the papers that were shoved at him.

"That will be all," the First Secretary concluded, "you should leave by the 10.30 a.m. flight. Good luck." He jerked his head to his companion and they left the room, shutting the door behind them.

Joe sat on the bed reading the prepared documents. He looked up when the bathroom door swung open. His Thai girl friend stood there before him naked as a new-born baby.

"What was that?" she asked huskily, coming towards him. "Must you always be dramatic?" Joe looked at his watch and grinned suddenly. "Not as dramatic as I will be in a moment," he laughed at her. He picked her up and deposited her on the bed.

* * *

"It was an act of destiny that we have been working together," Jack Edmonds told Simons, who sat dumbly before him. Caesar Oscar and Wogslav Jamicsz were also present at the briefing. They were in an underground cellar in one of the seedy parts of West 1 52nd Street in Washington D. C.

"An act of destiny and an act of fate," Jack repeated, gazing intently into Simons' face. Sweat trickled down the broad forehead of the latter. His lips moved but he said nothing. "We protect all those who project us; we guarantee those who guarantee us," Jack was saying. "You know what we expect of you because you know us and we know you."

48

A tall, burly figure came into the room, carrying a tray of drinks. He put it down on the coffee table and went out of the room again.

"You may now think that you have all the powers in the world and you can come after us," Jack said to Simons. "But you will be making a big mistake if you assume that. One word from us and you are finished; not just finished but dead."

"I resent your tone and your language," Simons said with impotent anger. "I've always served you well. Why are you complaining?"

"I'm not complaining, my good friend. I'm merely stating the fact. We're ready to take over the rulership of the world and you will help us make that happen. You see, we have placed a lot of stake on you and the shape things will eventually take will depend on the role you play from today."

"You can count on me," Simons said quietly, gulping down his whisky.

"I know we can; that's why I called this meeting. Remember the new schedules and time-table and the new contact points. Follow them meticulously and all will be well. Deviate from them and...." He let the sentence hang, with unmistakable threat. "You can go now; we have a few other things to talk over."

Simons placed his glass on the table, gathered his coat from the arm of one of the chairs and left the room wearily, like a man who had just been told by his trusted doctor that he has cancer.

* * *

"Look at the map of the drugs world," the Nigerian President, Naku Chiba, told his foreign minister. They were discussing in the president's study in Aso Rock, Abuja. Without allowing his minister to respond to his poser, he continued. "The entire European, American and Asiatic belts are diseased. Drugs is the bane of their old civilization. Drugs -is going to be the crisis point of their development. Africa is spared the plague of the white powder."

"What has that got to do with your vision of a new Africa?" the minister asked.

"Plenty. Drugs will destroy Europe and America and a substantial part of Asia. Mark my words. Africa will inherit what

49

they will lose. We will do all we can to help check the drugs trade; but beyond that the process of degeneration has already become irreversible. When that is completed, Africa will be there to reap what is left; I'll be there also."

The minister almost laughed at the usual weekly sermon of his president. But he held himself in check just in time. For two reasons: one, because it would have been disrespectful, and two, the president had the uncanny gift of seeing things others fail to see. He reflected that almost everything Mr. President had ever told them - including the theories that sounded as absurd as the present one - had all come to pass. Better to watch out and see how things develop than ridicule himself by laughing at his leader's seemingly outlandish view.

Chapter Eight

The mid-day heat in Abu Dhabi was ferocious. The sun hung over the capital of the UAE as if permanently suspended there. There was stillness everywhere, save for the bustling of brightly clothed people pursuing their daily businesses and the incessant roar of traffic. People gathered in coffee shops, sipping their drinks and telling tales of their exploits. Nobody talked about the heat which had become a landmark.

But the Abu Dhabi Sheraton hotel was a contrast from the rest of the capital city. It was built on the outskirts of the city away from the numerous mosques in the city. It was well away from the statues of Mohammed and various other religious leaders. The hotel was different because it was well protected from the sun by tall, enormous plants. Its gardens were well terraced with cane chairs scattered here and there. The swimming pool area also had many tall plants except for a small sun-bathing space.

The interior of the hotel was lavish. It said a ht about the economic fortunes of the emirates, and their desire to attract as much of the world as possible. Bellhops carried suitcases and other belongings in trollies to the batteries of lifts in the lobby, saluting the guests who either made their way up or down the 16-storey structure.

The reception counter, which was made of polished marble, on which rested numerous computer terminals, was as busy as any 5-star hotel in an oil-rich emirate could be.

In suite 426 of the seventh floor, a conference of sorts was taking place. From the hushed tones of the discussion and the studied relaxation of the men inside, one could see that the matter at hand was really very grave. None of the men was what he claimed to be, and none had journeyed to Abu Dhabi with genuine papers except for Sheik Abdulla Rhaman.

Abu was the principal operator in the fast burgeoning trade in hard drugs in the Gulf region. The others came in fake names. Jack Edmonds had transformed himself into Peter Donalds, a visiting oil prospector with a legally registered oil company financed and controlled by the consortium.

Caesar Oscar had suddenly become Eduordo Alarez, an international financier interested in the real estate business. Lady Barbara Alumineza was appropriately dressed as the wife of Sheik Abu, down to her white veils and heavy clothing. Even Sheik Abu's identity was very suspicious because his papers described him as a broker from one of the lesser emirates that made up the UAE. Guttfried Von Guttingberg feigned as Ferdinand Matthews, a high-flying businessman interested in international maritime trade, while Friedreich D'Armes had valid papers that described him as a Swedish investor interested in the new petro-chemical plant being built by the UAE government.

There were left overs of orange juice and continental breakfast on the portable trolley, in addition to the jugs of ice water and cubes. The time was a few minutes past eleven o'clock in the morning.

"Lady and Gentlemen," Jack Edmonds began, "we all know why we are here. Things are really happening and we must not only keep abreast of events; we must dictate the tune of the times using the tactics and strategies we have already mapped out. For starters, you all have been informed about the appointment bf Simons as the new anti-drugs scum of Washington."

"That is welcome news but we cannot rely on that as we cannot rely on the other heroes of darkness who want to arrest the light we want to bring to civilised humanity."

He paused suddenly, reached for his glass of orange juice and gulped it down quickly. He looked out through the drawn blind and contemplated the rapidly moving vehicles for a while. Then he turned back to his colleagues in the room and continued in the same measured tone.

"There are a number of reports that we must take; then we will work out the time-table for the implementation of the Central Committee's decisions." He looked sideways at Guttingberg who placed his glass of juice on the table and cleared his throat.

"The seven operations went very well. The first shipment was through the Gulf of Agwaba. The second came by the straits of

Hormuz. Both have been dispersed in arms catchment safe housed in Turkey, Cyprus, Lebanon and Qatar. They will take care of our Mid-East, Mediterranean and North-European operations. The third and fourth shipments came through the Spanish port. The Customs officials there were splendid. The arms are safe as could be and ready to be put to immediate use. The last three shipments covered the Asian and South American regions and are safe in the hands of the local commanders. The new recruits are all doing well, but the multiplicity of command structures is giving everybody a serious headache. I suggest that this meeting appoints a commander-in-chief of the entire forces, taking into consideration he developed structures our friends in the Golden Triangle, Colombia and the peninsular have."

"Brothers and sister," Jack Edmonds said, "you have all heard or yourselves. Lady Barbara, it's your turn next." Lady Barbara arched her eyebrows and laid her well-manicured fingers on her laps. As usual, there was a far away inscrutable look in her eyes. Her attitude was one of considered deliberation and they knew well not to hurry her. She was a. woman who liked to take her time in everything she did.

"There are a number of complications," she began in her sonorous voice. 'Perhaps, you know that the National Security Ministers of the EEC met recently in Paris under Washington's prodding."

She glanced at the blank faces around he, and decided to continue, "The meeting was about us, what we are and who we are and how to stop us. Their information is still sketchy but they know that a consortium exists and is interested in political power, through armed insurrection."

Sons of the men shifted in their seats. The Shiek's face was craned forward, fascinated by her words.

"They have decided to set up a joint European anti-drugs commission to be headed by the French head of state security. They are recruiting agents all over Europe. They are also vaguely aware of the arms transactions and are beginning to suspect our involvement in the American First Bank Shares - from information supplied by Washington, I presume."

She opened her handbag and brought out the tiny disc she had retrieved from Jean Jacques a few days earlier. This she gave to Jack Edmonds. "This is the verbatim recording of the Minister's deliberations," she said. Edmonds took the disc from her, opened a cigarette case and put it there.

"Thank you, the one and only Lady Bardara. You have done very well. Well, brothers, you have heard all. It seems that we have not been as careful as we ought to be. I propose that we do the following without delay. One, we should withdraw quietly from First Bank Shares. It's a process that will take a couple of months if we are to avoid suspicion. We should seek alternative channels for the movement of our funds. At the end of this period, not before, we should consider Anthony Roberts expendable and place a prize on him."

"Secondly, we should move our operational headquarters from New York to one of the smaller European cities. I'll make that choice very soon. Thirdly, we should appoint General Javierkez Dos Santus as the supreme commander of all our forces and Generals Karl Von Kutz and Thong Wongo as his deputies. We should also speed up our operations now. A time-table and tactical committee should be set up to stream-line our engagements and to work out the appropriate time we should commence our political operations. Any questions?"

There were none. He looked around and nodded.

"I'll be sending you the transcript of this recording in a few days' time. Lady Barbara and Guttingberg should be commended for their work. Keep it up."

The meeting broke up soon after that and the men left the room at an interval of about ten minutes to avoid any suspicion. Lady Barbara remained behind in the room to do further non-business consultation with Jack Edmonds.

* * *

Joe Lucas was not very happy with his flight to Washington, D.C. Not that the flight itself was bad, far from it. It was among the best that he had ever had. The food was good and the hostesses charming. Yet, he was terribly bothered about his new assignment. Bothered not because of the danger; that had already become second nature to him. But bothered because of the character of his new boss, knowledge of which he alone possessed and which he had kept to himself.

He knew Simons very well, being a product of the CIA himself and being only "loaned" to the DEA just two years ago. The Simons he knew was ambitious and unscrupulous and not particular about how he got his reward and promotion. He was his station chief in Saigon, Phuom Penh, Madrid and Caracas. They didn't get on well; but that was beside the point. What bothered him was the unexplained disappearance of a Khemer Rouge partisan held by the CIA and the sudden escape of a Soviet spy in Madrid when Simons was the station head. In each case, he was the officer in-charge of the operation. In each case, Simons had been unable to explain his role in the two escapes. Even as a DEA man, he had heard stories from his underworld informants that Simons was neck deep in the drugs trade. Stories, any way, but the facts added up. To make such a man the boss of a larger-than-life anti-drugs operation was akin to asking the devil himself to conduct a choir. But the bastards in Washington could not look beyond their noses; and so Simons had progressed to become the deputy director of the CIA.

He had to watch his steps, he surmised, admiring the air hostess that just walked past him. He wouldn't put anything beyond the ambitious smart alecs, granted that the new stories were true. He would be prepared when he got to Washington, he told himself; prepared to expose the lie that was Washington's decision in due course. Somewhat reassured by this thought, he jerked his economy class seat further back, lay his head on the soft cushion and prepared to snatch some sleep.

* * *

The persistent ringing of the telephone woke General Javierez from has deep slumber. He stretched out his hand and reached for the receiver. "Yes," he shouted hoarsely, wondering who was calling. "Good morning, brother," Jack Edmonds' voice announced to him. "Get ready and meet me in Caracas in three day's time. The Hotel Acapulco. Come prepared for you will be assuming control of our entire forces.

"Yes Sir," he blurted out, the sleep leaving his eyes. He replaced the receiver and grinned to himself. As the commander of the Cali cartel forces, he had come a long way since being thrown out of the Colombian army six years back, but to hear the voice of the legendary Jack Edmonds was beyond his wildest imagination. Though a commander of the Cali forces, he was in contact with the Medellin and other drugs cartels and they all respected him. It dawned on him that he wouldn't have been so appointed unless the other cartels approved it. It therefore meant that he was a popular choice, and that if the stories he had lately heard were true, he would soon head not just the drugs forces, but be the commander-in-chief of an entirety new universal army that was poised to remake the world. Thoroughly refreshed by this joyful thought, he whistled happily to himself as he made his way to the toilet.

Chapter Nine

It was raining continuously. The pavements were wet and puddles of water formed in the numerous potholes on the sidewalk. The streets were wet too, so were the cars that flashed past, unmindful of the rainfall, their tyres throwing up showers of water on both sides of the road. Pedestrians cursed when the water hit them, otherwise they were engrossed in their business, covered as they were by layers of thick clothing and mackintoshes.

Joe Lucas hurried along the wet pavement. He was already late for his appointment with Simons. The Customs activity at JFK was very brief; he had a welcoming party of faceless but important government officials who whisked him away before embarrassing questions could be asked. The ride from the airport was very smooth and easy till the men dropped him off at the corner of East 62nd Avenue with the explanation that was as far as their order allowed. Joe was not perturbed in the least. Neither was he suspicious. The company acted in such manner, allowing the agent to make his way to his appointment unhindered. He grinned at their unsmiling faces and waved them goodbye.

From then, the journey became less than smooth. He got snarled in the downtown Washington D.C. streets and matters were made worse by the pelting rain. Now, he was very close to the subway and was hurrying to catch the 12.30 p. m. train that would take him to within walking distance to Simons' new office. A train hooted in the distance and he could hear the sound of its engine as it hurried to a stop. He increased his pace.

After a distance of fifty meters, he looked casually over his shoulders. About twenty meters away from where he was, he saw a loudly dressed men trudging along ostensibly towards the station. He wore a yellow and blue windcheater under his unbuttoned overcoat. He had check trousers and a brightly coloured canvass shoes. On. He was hatless and had no umbrella. His head was bowed to the driving rain and he gave no sign that he was disturbed in the least by the inclement weather.

Joe slowed his strides, his mind alert. He had seer the same figure when he came ou1. of the last taxi that brought him within a walking distance to the station. He did see the same figure also about ten minutes back. And here he was again, at exactly the same distance from where he was. He slowed down to a crawl. The man also slowed down, maintaining the same space between them. Joe grinned to himself, his fingers caressing the Smith and Weston that snuggled comfortably in his shoulder hoister.

They could see the subway from where he was and he mass of human activity going on there intrigued him. People dashed in and out of the station clutching their briefcases and handbags. A number of train coaches were also available and there was a lot of human traffic. He looked back from the corner of his eyes and saw that the distance between him and his considerably.

He looked ahead of him a d patched the thick crowd closely. Resting his head on he trunk of a tree not far away from the station house was a tail, burly man. He had an umbrella over his head while he held a newspaper with his other hand. His movements were casual and deliberate, too deliberate for either somebody about to board a train or waiting for another to arrive. Joe was not quite sure but he thought that he saw the man in the windcheater nod to the man reading the paper who had just glanced up and had given him a sidelong look.

On the other side of the road, across the rail tracks, a third man was approaching Joe rapidly, his eyes darting about him and the wild hair plastered on his forehead giving him a nightmarish look. He knew an ambush when he saw one, having been in many before and having set them for many others. But Joe was always alert and ready. He made took a detour and diverted to the left towards the shed where hawkers displayed their wares. Beyond the empty space was a cluster of old coaches. Between the open space and where he was, the surge of human activity was quite heavy. He felt confident that he was still safe. The man who leant on the tree trunk had left his post. Joe saw the closed umbrella resting on a tree trunk. The three· men came out, and throwing pretence away, converged on him.

Joe quickened his pace and was soon among the crowd at the

edge of the open space. When he was on the edge of the crowd, he pulled out his gun and fired in the air. The sound of the bullet coincided with the rumble of the thunder. People lay flat on the ground. That is, people minus the three stalkers. Joe steadied his aim and squeezed the trigger. The bullet caught one of the men high on the forehead where he stood gazing blankly at the scattered mass of people. He dropped to the ground with a groan. A shot whizzed past Joe's head and he broke into a run. He took a flying dive and gained access to the first train coach. He lay flat on the wet, muddy floor and peered out of a side of the coach.

He saw the second man - the one who had been tailing him for a long time - making his way to the clump of bushes on the left and fired a shot at him. The man swerved, threw his arms up and blundered inside the bush. Then more gunfire erupted and a piece of iron was chipped off some millimeters from his head. He raised his hand and fired rapidly, swinging his arm slowly. He heard a sound that soothed his nerves; the moaning sound of somebody who was hit. The figure rose from the ground, his bloodied arm extended, clutching a gun. He swayed on his feet. Joe shot him on the chest as he went down. Their companion fired blindly towards the train, his shots missing Joe by a wide margin. Joe replied with bang after bang. There was sudden stillness, except the screaming of children and women and the hoarse shouts of the men. The hired killer waited for a while and then began running towards the mass of humanity, his gun raised high and his aim wild.

Joe grinned to himself and rose to his feet. In the distance, he heard the sound of police sirens, and smiled again. "It's been quite a day," he thought, "quite a welcome to dear old Washington."

Simons looked at Joe Lucas for a moment and then smiled suddenly. Joe thought he detected a carefuxlly guarded look of disappointment on his boss' face when he came in. It was almost as if he was surprised to see him.

"Welcome old boy," Simons said. "How's Bangkok?" "Thank you, Sir," Joe replied. "Good old Bangkok was okay when I left it. Pardon me for the wetness. I had a little welcoming party near the subway on West 72nd street.

"What happened?" Simons asked, alarmed.

"A couple of goons took a liking to my face and my briefcase and decided that they wanted them. Two down and I'm sure the police caught the third."

"This may not be so simple," Simons added. "The coincidence is abnormal." Joe Lucas shrugged his shoulders. He knew that his cover had already been blown wide open and that the man sitting opposite him may be responsible. But that will sort itself out later, he thought. The important thing was to stay healthy and alive.

"I'll send one of our chaps to check with the local police. In the meantime, I want to fill you with some of the details you need."
The next two hours was given to a comprehensive briefing on the drugs business, sources and major routes, important cartels and their known leaders, channels of distribution in the States and the finances houses suspected of being involved in drugs money laundering.

* * *

The voice was very harsh. Simons was sweating profusely and held the telephone receiver close to his ears. He was alone in his house and had scrambled his call. "You always pride yourself about your genius," he screamed on the receiver, "you always accuse me of being a coward, but you cannot do a goddam thing properly. Imagine letting him go like that. This chap will bow the whole operation sky high, mark my words."

"Take it easy," the voice at the other end of the line said. Take it easy. The message only got through about twenty minutes after he came in and we never had enough time to set a proper trap. And don't be afraid..."

"Don't be afraid," Simons laughed, "when I'm alone here. You are safe while I'm exposed. That boy is bright. You have raised his suspicion."

"He may be bright; but there is nothing he can do. There is nothing anybody can do to us; not even the cowardly president of your country. We are set, and before they even know what is happening, it will be all over. Calm down"

The connection was broken. Simons looked at the half glass of whisky in his hand. His face had a smoldering look. His eyes glittered. Suddenly, he flung the glass into the fireplace. He stormed out of the sitting-room to his bedroom.

Joe Lucas lay down on the warm mattress of the 8-spring bed in a very obscure hotel in the seedy part of downtown Washington. It was a rule that no agent on undercover assignment ever disclosed his temporary abode. In his own case, he had more cause to remain anonymous. He had applied his expert disguise when he left Simons' office in a theatrical shop owned by a long-time friend. He was certain that he was not tailed, but had even taken the additional precaution of doing a merry-go-round across Washington.

He considered the events of the day and smiled ruefully. To be given a near hopeless assignment, and to have one's cover blown even before he made his first move would be a nightmare for several people. But not Joe Lucas. He liked challenges and this was the greatest of them he had ever faced. He stretched himself languidly, looking at the dirty ceiling.

His best bet was to turn the hunter into the hunted and will begin with his boss. He will call in all his reserves, built up over seventeen years of undercover work and they would begin work immediately. It will be interesting what they will discover; whether his boss was the man he suspected to be or just another greedy patriot who could do a deal with an insignificant enemy agent to augment his meagre salary. That would be quite interesting, he speculated, shutting his eyes slowly.

Chapter Ten

The city of Caracas was as busy as ever. Near the tomb of the ancients the huge water fountain cascaded over rolling stone steps and all around the large sunken bath. Tourists gathered in droves, gazing at the tomb and occasionally allowing the cascading water to distract them. Traffic was heavy.

A medium-sized man in tourist attire with a camera flung over his shoulder, began to walk away from the tomb, winding his way to the fountain. He stood very close to the edge of the low wall that circled the water fountain and gazed at the tiny geysers of the falling water.

"Such a warm day," a voice spoke quite close to his ears.
He looked up sharply and saw the smiling face of a short, thin man dressed in a pin-striped suit, looked the man over for a full minute, imprinting his face in his memory. Then, his face split into a broad grin.

"Such a warm day, friend," he finally replied. "The water is as blue as ever." The thin man looked around them in a casual way, brought out a parcel and thrust it into the hand of the supposed tourist. Then, without saying another word, he began to walk towards the busy road and was soon swallowed up by the thick crowd.

General Javierez Dos Santus shoved the parcel inside the side pocket of his sports shirt and continued gazing at the splash of the ever-rising and falling water. Five minutes later, he left the vicinity of the tomb and the fountain and began to walk down the road - in the opposite direction to which the other man went -towards the Hotel Acapulco, a distance of about three hundred meters from the tomb.

* * *

Jack Edmonds and Caesar Oscar were finishing their lavish supper when a knock came on the door of the former's hotel suite. Caesar Oscar picked up his gun from the table and holding it behind him, walked to the door. He peered through the peephole and unlatched the chain from the door. Then he turned the round handle slowly.

Javierev Dos Santus stooa outside the door, his face bland and his hands still by his sides.

"Welcome to Caracas," Caesar said, leading him inside the room. "I guess you have met Mr Edmonds before?" he asked him, offering him a seat by the occasional table in the living-room.

"Not physically, I regret, but his reputation precedes him. I'm honoured in your presence," he added, offering a handshake.
Jack Edmonds gripped his h8nd very warmly, saying at the same time, "There is always time to meet and time to have stories. Now is the time to meet. Make yourself comfortable."

"What would you drink?" Caesar asked him. "We have whisky, Martini, French Cognac and Sherry."

"Cognac will be good."

While Caesar Oscar busied himself getting the drinks, Edmonds opened his briefcase and brought out a thin file folder. He placed it on the table and snapped the briefcase shut, which he placed by his side again. Dos Santus watched silently, trying as much as he could to look intelligent and active. Caesar came back with a bottle of Hennessey and a short glass which he placed by Dos Santus' side.

"Ice cubes?" he asked. "No, I prefer it straight."

Caesar Oscar smiled silently to himself. The experienced General was truly himself, which was a good sign. Other people in his position would have asked for ice cubes, at least to show that they are cultured and know the modern way of life. But he was aware that no real Latino ever drank Cognac with ice cubes, particularly a tough warlord like Dos Santus.

"Well, General," Edmonds began. "Let's get to the real issue why we are here. We have studied your dossier closely, scrutinised your credentials and assessed your commitment to the cause." Edmonds said this while tapping the file folder in front of him. "We have no doubt that you are the kind of man we want, a man with a ruthless dedication to duty, grim determination and will to achieve results and a man with total commitment to set objectives."

"I'm very flattered," the General murmured.

"The job at hand is not a flattering one," Edmonds said lightly.

"You are the engine of our new, universal army, the man on whose shoulders lies the burden of remaking the world according to our image, at least in the military sphere. Such a job is most challenging. That, of course, you know."

General Dos Santus bowed his head slightly, as if to show that he knew the enormous responsibilities placed on his head.

"I'll do my best," he said softly. "You can count on me. I'll never disappoint the consortium. I place my life on that expectation."

"I am glad to hear that. Your assignment is to compile a confidential report on the various armed formations that presently exist in the various cartels. Troop strength, level of training, exposure and experience." Edmonds paused and glanced at some of the sheets of paper in the file folder.

"Your second assignment is to take an inventory of all the arms at our disposal, catalogued according to the various formations. Next, you will liaise with Guttfried Von Gottingberg for the full details of our recent purchases. At the political level, he is our co-ordinator of military affairs, and though you have absolute discretion over purely military matters, the political decisions reside with his committee."

"An advance notice will be sent to him," Caesar Oscar added.

"You will be briefed on when and how to contact him."

"Lastly," Edmonds concluded, "You'll be required to prepare a comprehensive report on how to integrate the various units into a centralised fighting force, and work out the necessary tactics and strategies for our imminent operations."

He gathered the papers in the file folder together and gave them to Dos Santus. "Study these in detail and bring them back to me later this afternoon."

Dos Santus stood up and as if inspired by some hidden force, saluted Jack Edmonds as a soldier will his Commander-in-Chief. He began to walk towards the door.

"Lest I forget," Edmonds added when Dos Santus turned.

"Your deputies are Generals Karl Kutz and Thong Wongo of the Free European Enterprises and the Golden Triangle Bloc respectively. They will be in touch with you very soon."

The door snapped shut behind the elated General and the two men went back to their drinking which his entry had interrupted.

* * *

"Get the Director of the National Drugs Agency for me," the president, Nuka Chiba, told his personal assistant. "I want him to see me at 6 o'clock this evening." The aide looked up from the table and regarded his boss quizzically. The Drugs Agency was under the Internal Affairs Ministry and it was unusual that its Director - a not-to-highly placed official - should be summoned to meet with the president on such a short notice. But he knew well not to question his boss' judgement, as numerous solid and logical reasons would be immediately proffered to justify his action. The aide, a dynamic young man in his early forties, had come to trust and count on the intellect and vision of his boss and had come to admire the man's foresight, even when some of his decisions might have initially appeared far-fetched or even outrightly eccentric.

The Director of the NDA came into the president's office that evening, doing very little to stop the trickle of sweat that ran down his shirt from the base of his neck. Sweat beads also covered his forehead. He had repeatedly dabbed at them while waiting in the outer office and had finally given up further efforts. An experienced police officer, he earned his present position purely on the strength of his records. He knew enough about politics to understand that he had numerous enemies who would gladly flay him alive and eat his flesh and wondered how he had stepped out of time. Meeting the president of one's country, face to face, not to talk of privately, he reflected, was no ordinary phenomenon. Because of his conventional wisdom, he readily imagined that no such summons could come without some foreboding.

Sit down Mr. Tupa," the president said, "and make yourself much at home." Then he smiled at the trembling officer. President Nuka Chiba had a way of putting people at ease and relaxed in his presence. He did that now.

How is the job going?" he suddenly asked, picking up a piece of paper from his desk. He glanced at it for a moment and put it away.

"Feel free to give me your candid opinion; not the routine stuff

65

that you pass on to gratiate your superiors." He smiled at Tupa again.

"Well, Your Excellency, where do I begin?" he started. "Our main problem has remained inadequate financing and lack of equipment. Beyond that, however, I cannot guarantee the integrity of some of the chaps; those high up in the office and those in the field. Some of them are highly connected and the drugs barons pull a lot of weight. Very few people will tell you this, but I want to state it as plainly as possible."

The president vigorously nodded several times, tapping his gold pen on his teeth.

"Is it possible to raise a formidable force of "untouchables", capable of running the place the way you and I want it done?" he asked.

"In principle, Sir, that will be possible, but I'll not get the free hand to restructure and professionalise the place. Many people, some of them very close to you, will call for my head."

"That is understandable, but things have changed. Listen carefully. I want you to re-organise the NDA as thoroughly as possible. Make any decisions you dim fit. You'll have complete independence in this assignment. I'll inform the Minister about my decision. But first, prepare a blue-print of what we need. Have it sent to my office without delay. I'll have it approved. Another thing, let this discussion not leave this office."

"You can count on me, Sir," Tupa replied breathlessly, hardly believing his ears. "I'll start right away."

"If things go the way I think they wilt, that unit will play a vital role in the survival of this country and the future of mankind."

Mr Tupa stood up and thanked the president again. "Have you studied the recent drugs man of the world?" The question came as if from nowhere. Tupa was thrown off his guard.

"Why, yes Sir."

"If you have, South Africa is completely missing from the drugs routes and transit centres. But that is where, I understand, our drugs chaps have made their new haven. Have that checked out and include it in your report."

Tupa hesitated for a moment, marvelling at the president's astonishing grasp of even the minutest details. He left the room quickly, clicking the door shut as he went.

"Get me the Internal Affairs Minister on his private line" the president told his Personal Assistant on the Intercom." "I have an urgent message for him." His aide assured him that he would do that right away. "Something is going to happen very soon," he mused.

* * *

"How is the new anti-drugs outfit doing?" the president asked Chris Williams of the CIA during the Weekly Security briefing. All eyes turned to Chris. He cleared his throat loudly and adjusted his wrist watch.

"So far, so good," he said. "Simons is doing a good job. He has assembled his team. Documents are being studied and top-level contacts discreetly made with out European, South American and Asian partners. Things are generally moving in the right direction. We will have something concrete in the next couple of weeks."

"Well, tell them not to take all the time in the world," the president added with a smile. "There are independent sources of drugs information and the situation report is getting worse daily."

Williams was startled. He had thought that Simons' agency would be the only source of information through him - to the White House. People were already squealing, especially people who never liked him and his choice of Simons as the director of the elite agency. He had to tell the bastard to hurry up and produce results quickly. The whole thing had totally gone off his mind and he only just remembered about Simons and his new outfit when the president posed his question.

"Incorporate the report as part of your weekly briefing." He was aware that the President was talking.

"I'll take care of that, Sir," he said dispiritedly.

"That alters my initial plan of giving Simons unlimited access to the White House." Williams nodded, suspecting that something had gone wrong somewhere. He thought about it and decided that it was in the nature of his boss to change his mind without warning.

Chapter Eleven

Lerec was a thoroughbred professional. He had been for the past sixteen years. A special agent of the OU D'Quaissy, the deadliest unit of the SDECE, he had seen action in counter-espionage abroad and counter-insurgency at home. He was a special trainee in one of France's elite spy school when Carlos the Jackey, operating in the Latin Quarters of Paris, in the mid-70s, shot two special agents and a Lebanese terrorist before making his escape to the unknown.

Since that incident, Lerec had decided to make the underworld his quarry, gathering as much information about it as possible and establishing wide-ranging contacts with its principal and minor characters. In his decade and half as a special agent, he had come into contact with members of the organised crime syndicates, lone gangsters, pimps, professional paid killers, drugs barons and couriers and the general flotsam and jetsam that populated the seedy and rundown parts of many a European capital.

He had come to understand the inner workings of the criminal mind, the various operational strategies of major drugs cartels and the secret behind the numerous successes of the various crime groups. He had sometimes respected the time-honoured conventions and rules of the underworld when they didn't contradict his present assignment, but had at other times moved brutally against them, regardless of who was the sponsor.

It, therefore, came as no surprise to him when he was informed by his boss that the French Minister of Internal Affairs and National Security wished to speak to him about a special assignment that bordered on national security. On meeting with Jean Jacques D'Atmand, he learnt that he had been appointed a special agent to oversee a pan-European anti-drugs operation, and he was to work closely with his opposite number in the USA.

He had impressed the Minister with his knowledge of the world-wide trade in drugs, the sources of the various narcotic products, the routes used by couriers, the major drugs cartels, and the pay-off system that corrupted both security agents and public officers. Jean Jacques nodded repeatedly as Lerec marshalled his points and was particularly happy that he had made what he called "a brilliant presentation."

Lerec had set to work immediately, contacting the various anti-drugs agencies in Europe and hemming in numerous dossiers on special field agents whom he will eventually use as his special squad. In no time, he had put together a special group of dedicated agents from over fourteen European nations while he maintained a core staff of five in France itself. In less than no time, he had activated his extensive networks and scrutinised thousands of documents on drugs-related issues.

After two weeks of breathless and intensive activity, an idea came to his mind, the idea of a new drugs source that was stronger than most people may have previously thought, with its consequences for Europe, USA and most parts of South America and Asia. At the centre of this degenerate business was a supercartel. He had reasoned it out and felt sure of his facts. He felt that the new global supercartel advanced in technology seemed to be operating from wherever that suited its fancy at very short notice.

Then, he got his first break. An untraceable call was picked up at the Marseilles office of his special unit. The caller, who refused to identify himself, merely stated that he had information to sell at a certain price because he wanted to get out, for as he put it, "these chaps are bad, real bad." The fellow in charge of the office hesitated. They usually received such calls and most often, the package that would eventually be delivered never amounted to anything. He asked to know why the "office" should be interested in such an exchange.

The man's uneven breathing came across clearly over the phone. Finally, he replied: "You are wasting time. How come I know this number? I also know that Mr Lerec is in charge of your operations."

That was that. This piece of information shocked the officer in charge, named Tabuled. Only a very limited number of people knew about their existence and the fact that Lerec was in charge of the operations. That showed the power and reach of their invisible enemy, he surmised.

When he realised that the man was talking rapidly, he paused in his thoughts to get all the details about the exchange. The man never survived the exchange, for his body was fished out of the waters of the Marseilles wharf, but the package was recovered. Its information was sketchy but is established that there existed a supercartel overseeing the global drugs trade, that it initially operated from somewhere in Brooklyn, New York and its leader was powerful and respected all over America and Europe. The package further contained information that the central objective of the supercartel was to weaken the moral and social fibre of a number of the American, European, Asian and Arab States, as a prelude to their political and military conquest.

Lerec was overjoyed with the information at his disposal and the number of tentative leads that had suddenly opened up. He felt that such information adequately compensated for his blown cover, which in itself was a very serious security risk for it showed that there was a dangerous leak high up in the hierarchy of the government or probably the governments of their European allies. Thorough enquiries were made and it was discovered that the dead man was a Colombian who belonged to the Medellin cartel. It was also learnt from scraps of paper found in a waterproof punch he concealed on his thigh that he was disillusioned with the death of Pablo Escobar; an act he attributed to betrayal by the drugs barons. He claimed that they now paid lip-service to the dead man's name, using it only as a spring board to further their globalist intention. He wanted to get out and had struck a deal with the new force being put together to hunt all the drugs producers and dealers.

It seemed that he had made a terrible mistake as he was being shadowed without his knowing it. Though his call was traced, he still had enough time to place the package where he said it would be. He had not waited to make the contact because paid killers were hot on his heels. He managed to get to the wharf and was arranging a boat at the water-front when they struck. The chaps at the Marseilles office, it was eventually revealed, came to the scene barely ten minutes after the killers had escaped.

Lerec was now ready to make his first move. He knew the danger it involved because of his blown cover but he was not unduly worried. He was always capable of taking care of himself. It was his contact that he feared for but he trusted in his experience of many years. He had set the appointment by "blind" couriers who never suspected what was afoot and whose credibility was double-checked at every turn of the process. Then he had waited a week for something to happen. Nothing did. After another week of anxious waiting he decided that it was safe enough to make his move.

Rue de Quassy was a disreputable part of Paris, where most of the rundown night-clubs and bars and the worst kind of prostitutes, pimps, con men, cut-throats are located. It was always gloomy because of the shabby over-hanging branches of the trees that lined its potholed thoroughfare and the stolen bulbs from the street lights.

It was late evening when Lerec got down from a virtually broken down taxi driven by a sour-faced character with decayed teeth at a corner of the street. He looked around him casually, hunched his shoulders against the biting cold and joined the noisy mass of people that crowded the side-walk.

Prostitutes hung at all corners of the street, their faces heavily made up and their over-exposed body unmindful of the driving cold. Pimps lunged farther back in the thickening shadows, their hands inside their coat or trouser pockets, gripping either a gun, a knife, a chain or a crow bar. Drunken men floated along and fights broke out regularly. Most of the bars had already come alive and the sound of pop music could be heard from their neon-plastered entrances from where people spilled in and out.

Lerec moved unhurriedly, his eyes scanning the pressing gloom and his hands thrust very deep in his coat pockets, the right one gripping his service pistol. He came to a gloomy four-storey building on which ground floor there was a tobacconist's shop; and he paused slightly. People streamed past him, some gazing emptily at the building while others wrangled about something or the other.

He resumed his walk, slowing his pace considerably. He was almost close to his destination. From a darkened doorway ahead of him, a white handkerchief was casually thrown out. He glanced at his watch and nodded. He quickened his pace and went past the door way. Behind him, he heard soft footfalls. He looked over his shoulder and the man behind him nodded. He slowed down till the man walked up to him.

The man was a grey-haired fellow in his late fifties whose scarred face and glistening eyes spoke of innumerable intrigues, conspiracies and fights. He was tall and skinny but carried himself with a dignified, stiff alertness. He wore a shabby suit and his shoes looked old from use. All the same, he was neat; at least neater than most of the characters Lerec had already met at Rue De Quassy.

The man was Joannes Febrae, half-German and half-French and he had lived all his life in Rue de Quassy. May be, lived is not a correct word, but he had existed there for as long as Lerec could remember and could be 'considered one of its major landmarks. A con-man, drug pusher, dealer in stolen goods, a part-time pimp several years earlier and retired paid killer, he knew all about the underworld and had struck a peculiar relationship with Lerec who had once made sure that he was convicted on a minor charge of receiving stolen goods.

They walked down the street silently and branched off on the right to a narrow alley that was considered pert of Rue de Quassy. They paused at the open space in front of a busy cafe where tables and chairs were laid out and went in. They sat on the rickety chairs, drawing their chairs sideways so that they could watch the entrance to the open space.

A dirty waiter came to their table and took their order. When he went away, they relaxed visibly. Lerec extended his hand and Febrae shook it wearily. "Long time no see, Pal", he said. "I thought the bad boys finally got you." "Well, you see I'm still alive and well," Lerec replied, "and hope to stay so."

The waiter came back with their order of coffee and went away. They remained silent till he was out of earshot. Their table was quite isolated, the nearest one to it, around which a group of men argued hoarsely being about three meters away.

"Let's make this meeting as brief as we can," Febrae said. "It's sheer poison talking to you. The boys will love it."

What do you know about the new superdrugs cartel that operates out of New York and which seems to have a global reach?"

Febrae took his time in answering. "What made you so interested in them now?'" he asked.

'Never mind that. Just tell me what you know. These boys are as polished as gem and as deadly as a wounded rattlesnake," he said.

"They are not exactly new, being the incarnation of the major drugs cartels; .a solid alliance if I may add. They operated out of the Brooklyn area - district unknown - till lately. I'm informed that they have dismantled their Brooklyn operations."

"Who are their known leaders?"

"Who can tell the known leaders of such a group? Check the list of the leaders of the major drugs cartels and you ascertain their leaders."

"That will not help," Lerec said. "For one thing, others may be fronting for them in the new Council; and for another, it's a cumbersome task. A central council makes their decision for them. Who are in that council? You must know, so don't hedge."

Febrae smiled thinly. "You credit me with enormous powers. I wish I had them." Then, he remembered his early years in Germany and his close friendship with Guttfried Von Guttingberg, a ruthless and very ambitious man, then new in the drugs and killer-for-hire business. They had parted ways many years ago as their interest had diverged. He had not heard of Guttingberg again until lately when it was whispered that he was into something big; that he now belonged to a new super drugs organisation that was poised to take the world by storm. He hesitated. The expression was not lost on Lerec.

"Come on, Febrae, spill it. What do you have to lose?"

"Well, I may not be so sure, but there is a certain childhood friend who may or may not be one of the men you are looking for. We used to be very close many years ago. I think he may be your

73

man. His name is Guttfri..."

That was as far as Febrae got. Two shadowy figures had suddenly emerged from the cafe, one of them raised his pistol and shot him in the back of his head. Lerec saw the grey-haired man shudder and topple over. He kicked his chair aside and rolled to the floor as more gunfire broke out. A bullet nicked his forearm and a second took his hat clear off his head. He rolled several times on the concrete floor, toward the darkened end of the open space, his gun in his hand. He fired repeatedly. A bullet caught one of the men on the forehead and he slumped to the ground. The second killer rushed away from the cafe front, towards a mass of people walking down the alley, firing as he went. Lerec got to his feet slowly and walked to where Febrae lay. He touched the side of his neck and straightened up.

The gathered crowd backed away as the gun in his hand was still smoking. He brought out his radio receiver and placed an urgent call to his office.

Chapter Twelve

"What I've been telling you is that these people are real bastards," said Jonas, a wiry, bird-like men as he walked down the lush avenue that led to St. Peter's Church. It was a Sunday morning and worshipers were already thronging to the church for service.

They had agreed to meet there about three days earlier, and the arrangement had been difficult to make. Jonas had been open and evasive and wanted nothing to do with what he called Lucas' "lunatic and suicidal assignment." Eventually, he was convinced and agreed to meet him in the churchyard the next Sunday.

They blended well with the actual worshipers as they all dressed quite alike. They walked rather briskly, keeping pace with the other people that milled all around them.

"What makes you think that these people are real bastards?" Lucas asked, with a mischievous twinkle in his eyes.

"Ah, Mr Lucas, how can you say that? You know as well as I do what I'm talking about."

"What are you talking about? Drugs barons and dealers are desperate people; we all know that. What's so special in that?"

"Well, if you don't know, I can tell you. These are no ordinary pushers such as you read about in newspapers and magazines."

There was an agitated bent in Jonas' tone.

'These people- are members of a new generation of drug producers and dealers; they have a global outfit, a powerful network that changes with the punch of the computer button and an army that can overrun entire countries."

"I hope you have not been watching too many movies," Lucas said soberly.

"I never watch movies. Honest to God," the veteran informant said. "They deceive people. What I'm telling you is as real as you and I."

"You have not really told me anything that I can't find out for myself if I read the latest despatches in my office. What is new?" Jonas hesitated. He slowed down his pace and looked at Lucas intently. Jonas seemed to have made up his mind and when he began to speak, there was a far away look in his eyes, as if he was not addressing someone next to him.

Here then are the facts, Mr Lucas he said. "One, these people know who you are; have always known the moment you were picked for this job. How do you fight people about whom we know nothing when your cover has already been blown sky high? Two, your boss, Mr Simons is a principal character in this drama though neither you nor I can prove it. How can you achieve any useful result in your investigation when the man who gives you assignments and whom you report to may probably be a paid agent of the opposition? Third, two meetings went very badly in Paris barely a week ago. One was an exchange that was to take place in Marseilles. The informant was fished out of the water. They knew everything about him even before he picked up the phone to make the first call. The second was in Rue d'Quassy, Paris, and it was set up by your opposite number in Paris, Mr Lerec. The man he went to meet, just as you are now meeting me, was shot dead because he opened his mouth very wide. How' come these people know about the slain man, Mr Lerec and the fact that they have set up a meeting? And Febrae the dead man - was the best in our field. Better than myself. I respected that guy but see what these chaps have done to him." He bowed his head..."How am I certain that I'm safe even here?" he 'shouted out suddenly. "How am I sure that I've not already been sold to these bastards?"

"Take it easy," Lucas assured him, "you are safe once you stick very close to me. Now, tell me, how did you come about all this information?'

Jonas fondled his beard and there was a glint in his eyes. He smiled ugly.

"I'm a guy who gets to know things," Mr Lucas. And don't ask me about my source because you are not gona get that from me."

"Is that your final word?" he asked.

"Yes, if there is nothing more, Mr Lucas, I have things to do and staying alive and healthy is one of them."

"One more thing. How do I get a lead to these people? Surely, you must know something about some of these chaps or, at least, people who know who they are?"

"There is always your boss," Jonas said mischievously. "He could lead you to them:" He paused and began to reflect. "Then, you can check on the First American Bank Shares. I've heard that funny things do happen there. Find, out why one of its Vice-Presidents, Mr Peter Nicholson, was murdered. There is another man that could be of help to you. He's pretty deep in the Medellin connection. Bardi Orlando is the name. He is as dangerous as the core and quick with the knife or gun. He hangs out in Peppy's saloon in downtown Washington. Do not say that I sent you. That man's name is poison. Good bye Mr Lucas."

With that, he turned abruptly and began to walk towards the far end of the avenue towards the main road. He never looked back once. Lucas continued his walk to the church, pondering on the information he had gathered.

Jonas intrigued him. He had a wealth of information on the drugs business that would scare the entire DEA's computer data bank. He had met the man by accident one year ago during a drugs bust and had established a firm relationship with him during the trial. He had beat the rap because the prosecutor did a bad job, end their principal witness had disappeared. Since he came out of detention, Jonas had stayed clean -somewhat - and had become his occasional informant. He in turn had avoided his known hunts, warning him in advance about an impending raid. Through that way, both of them stayed alive and healthy.

He now had three principal leads. He would confront his boss but not directly. He knew that Simons never used the ordinary telephone. He used the portable telephone box that was easy to scramble. He would have a look at that box and some of its knobs. He had the bank investigation to contend with. But that would wait till he had settled the Simons problem. That would wait too till after he had called on Bardi Orlando at Peppy's bar. He still had a number of leads from the vague information that he had squeezed out of Simons in the office. A few of the guys he could trust were still deep in the field and it will take weeks for them to come up with something concrete. He still had to meet with that remarkable

French man, Mr Lerec. They both shared something in common as professionals. They had been exposed by their bosses or by very important people in their governments. They both wanted to stay alive.

He knew he would be kept quite busy in the next week and he therefore was prepared to settle scores with the enemies of his State, before they could do him in. Every day in the office, he got the impression that Simons saw him as a big threat and was plotting to incapacitate him permanently. He wouldn't allow that to happen. He intended to catch the other fellow before he was caught himself. He had done that before. He would do that again; that he knew for sure.

'It had been an interesting evening,' Lucas thought as he walked towards Peppy's bar. The time was 9.30 p.m. and the night was hot and close. He grinned at nothing in particular. His adventure in Simons' house had been very successful. He knew that Simons lived alone and that his wife and three kids were living in Philadelphia, a convenient arrangement that saved his marriage and his career. He had waited in a shadowy part of a side Street to observe Simons leave his house. 'He waited another thirty minutes and made his move. He did a professional job on the telephone which he saw in Simons' bedroom, so well hidden that an amateur would have missed it. He now had a listening device dropped in his hotel room and hoped that it would be active for a few days before Simons suspected that something was wrong with his telephone.

He was now a few meters away from Peppy's saloon and quickened his pace, the way night club patrons would on hearing the familiar sound of the juké-box. He pushed the swing door open and was confronted by the blast of music, loud conversation and cigarette fumes. The saloon catered mainly for Latinos but quite a number of decrepit-looking white people were there. The bar hostesses were brassy and skimpily clad. So were the waitresses. He pushed his way to the bar counter and ordered a rye drink. The barman was a rat-like fellow whose watery eyes blinked repeatedly. "Hello pal," Lucas said when he had been served, "where can I find brother Orlando? I have a business with him. For his benefit." The barman looked him over quickly and jerked his head in the direction of a side door at the middle of the rectangular saloon.

Lucas picked up his drink and went to a table near the door. The door was open and led to a narrow and gloomy corridor. He took a sip of the rye, watched the events around him, particularly the antics of a drunken bar hostess who was around. He stood up and walked casually to the door. The passage was lonely and free of human traffic. He could see a door at its end.

When he was close to the door, a figure materialised out of nowhere, as if by magic. He looked around and saw a trap door that had swung shut. He looked the man over and saw that he was a thick-set brawler, whose battered face spoke of innumerable bar fights.

"Hey pal, where do you think you are going?" he snapped in a frightened voice. "You are in the wrong part of town, bud."

"I have a business with Orlando," Lucas replied.

"I know all about Orlando's appointments. Get out." Just then, a knife flashed in his hand.

"Hey, take it easy," Lucas said, edging backwards. Then he suddenly tripped. He went on one knee, coiled himself and sprang.

His flying tackle caught the man on his knees and the knife dropped with a clatter. The man cursed silently. As he groped for the knife, his questing hand reaching for its handle, Lucas jumped him anti kicked him viciously on the head. The man toppled over. Another kick to the solar plexus flattened him. He lay limp on the floor. Nothing happened.

He got to the door, tried the handle and pushed it open. The room was fair-sized and a man sat behind a desk, with a piece of paper containing cocaine powder in front of him. He jerked up when he saw Lucas, his hand reaching for something under the desk.

"Take it easy, pal," Lucas said, showing him his pistol. The man brought his hand out slowly. Lucas leaned on the door and turned the lock, his eyes never leaving the man's surprised face.

"You Orlando?" he asked. The man said nothing. "You deaf or something?" Lucas added. He had little patience with him and knew that the only language such a man understood was force and violence. He went to the desk, sliding the gun till he held it by the barrel. "Hey, your roof is leaking, see drops of water," Lucas said. Glancing up. The man glanced up too. His jaw was a perfect target. He smashed the gun butt on his jaw and quite liked the pleasant sound of cracking bone. The man toppled over his chair and fell with a crash onto the floor. Lucas reached and hoisted him up. He sat him down heavily on the chair. A trickle of blood appeared at the corner of the man's mouth.

"You Orlando?" he repeated. The man nodded slowly with hatred in his eyes. "I have one question for you. You must give an answer. Who is the Medellin contact in the new drugs super cartel?" Orlando said nothing. Lucas slid the gun to its barrel and moved towards him again.

"Simpos Aseta," he spoke harshly. "He operates out of the Bronx in New York."

"May be you are lying. May be you are telling the truth. But I will refresh your imagination. He smacked Orlando with his clenched left fist on the face. He reeled back but did not topple over.

"Honest to God," he wailed. "He owns a tobacco shop in 152nd Avenue." Lucas was convinced.

"May be you will phone him to get away. May be you will arrange for him to be killed. But I'll come back for you again and when I do, you will regret your miserable life." He hit him again with the gun-butt, this time on the temple. His skin split open and he lay on the ground moaning.

Then, there was a loud bang on the door. A voice called out:

"Boss, are you okay?" More voices and bangs came. Lucas saw a window behind the desk, slid it open and jumped to the soft ground as a crash came on the door.

Chapter Thirteen

Jack Edmonds studied the papers in front of him, occasionally inclining his head and looking intently at particular details. He lay on a chair in front of the swimming pool in his Nassau holiday home. The water was deep blue and three beautiful ladies clad in the briefest of bikinis floated on its surface, their hair forming a free-flowing halo around their faces. They caused gentle ripples over the water surface and gentle lapping movements at the edges of the pool.

Jack Edmonds believed in living well, particularly after a very hard deal had been smoothly scaled. He didn't believe in families, and so he was unmarried. He wanted to devote his entire life to the cause," the philosophy of which he had already worked out in a number of papers, and the realisation of which he was now dedicated to.

The clinking of glasses in the upper sitting-room of the house, diverted his attention momentarily from the papers he was studying. He had too very important guests visiting at the moment and they would soon be needing his attention. He sighed softly and resumed his reading.

General Dos Santus had indeed done a superb job. He was impressed in spite of himself. He now had in his hands all the necessary details of all their men who were under arms, their present locations and combat-readiness and the areas from which more recruitment could be done. He also had details of the strategy and tactics of centralising their command structure and he nodded at the wily General's practical approach to issues. Most importantly, the meeting between Dos Dantus and Guttingberg had gone without hitch and the details of all the arms they possessed, from the most sophisticated rocket-launchers to the smallest bullet, were also provided.

There was so much to do and so little time to do them, he reasoned, but he liked challenges. They recreated and refreshed him, the way a good exercise or rest was wont to do. He glanced at the pool and saw the three ladies getting out of the water. They picked up their towels from the canvas decks on the side of the pool and began walking to the house, their buttocks rolling with the flow of their movement. He watched them till they got out of sight.

He would call a full council meeting soon, but had not yet decided on the venue. Apart from the immediate task at hand, there was the intimidating issue of the American Joe Lucas and the Frenchman Lerec. They were becoming very troublesome. The council would settle this little problem, and all the problems they may face till they conquered the whole world.

He got up from the reclining chair and walked to the house, clutching the papers.

* * *

Lerec had put aside the issue of his blown cover and the possibility of a dangerous leak in a powerful office in the government of his country for a while and concentrated on the urgent issue of identifying the Guttfri... whom Febrae had spoken about. It was as if the killers had been listening to their conversation and had moved in when it become very dangerous to their existence. He praised the men's professionalism. They had probably heard everything he had discussed with Febrae, which the surviving one would have passed to their paymasters, and they made sure that he never went home with anything substantial.

The incomplete name, Guttfri... intrigued him and he was determined to get at the man's full identity. He set to work and collected enormous amounts of information from his various sources. He had very close to thirty-six names of people in drugs or drugs-related businesses whose names had a Guttfri.... in them. It was quite some work, because some of them were just names. No addresses or other personal details were supplied. Yet, he plodded on, supplying faces and identities to the various names, eliminating those who were either dead or were couriers. He now had about eight names to go through and felt convinced that one of them was the man he was looking for, a German who had worked his way to the top hierarchy of the new drugs super cartel. He stretched himself in a chair in his office and yawned. He had been working for a long time and did not realise that it was getting quite late. His secretary and personal assistant had long gone but the three guards who circled the building, personally chosen by him, were still on their beat.

He had a briefing at the Internal Affairs Ministry to attend tomorrow by ten in the morning, and after that the joint meeting with his opposite numbers from Germany, Britain, Italy and Poland. He hoped to crack the mystery of Guttfri.... before then, or failing which his German colleague who had been very helpful with names arid other details relating to the mysterious man would have something for him. But he particularly looked forward to his meeting with the American agent, Joe Lucas, in a week's time. He had heard quite a lot about the incredible American agent and was impressed by his credentials. He was eager to work with him, a thoroughbred professional like himself.

He picked up his ballpoint and began making some notes on a pad in front of him, nodding gently as a particular detail or information struck .him as being very vital.

* * *

Simpos Ageta woke up with a start. There were sun patterns on the window panes, because the blinds were drawn. He glanced at the bedside clock and discovered that it was 6.56 a.m. He sighed, wiping the sweat on his forehead with the dainty bedclothes. His wife moved in her sleep, and looking at her, he thought that he would not see her again. Why he thought that way baffled and worried him because his morning appointment was just a routine, and had become such since he moved higher in the Medellin cartel and discovered that a new structure that would make all of them happy had been set up.

He got out of bed as gently as he could so as not to disturb her and went to the toilet just outside the door. His three little children slept in the other room which served as a sitting-room in the day. All this would change soon, he resolved, urinating inside the cracked toilet bowl. He had made enough money of late and had already saved enough to move to a three bedroom furnished apartment in a better part of the Bronx. He had gone to see the estate agent two days earlier and would seal the arrangement latter today after his appointment.

While in the toilet, he reflected on the message he had got the previous evening. It had come through the normal channel and he cross-checked its reliability. Everything matched. He was to collect a parcel from a man who would identify himself with certain code words at the trash dump towards the sea at 9 am the following morning and he was to send the parcel immediately to their special courier who would get it out of New York to Washington later that day. He knew the courier well, having dealt with him for over six years. He quite liked the man who appreciated his own sacrifices and devotion to the cause and had nothing but happiness for his progress.

His wife always surprised him. No matter how early he woke up, and how stealthily he crept out of bed, she was always waiting for him with his freshly laundered clothes and a cup of hot coffee and rolls.

This morning was no exception. A buxom woman in her mid-thirties, she bustled about the shabbily furnished room, getting things ready for him. Before 8 O'clock, he was quite ready to go, as the distance from his apartment to the trash dump was twenty minutes' brisk walk. He intended to walk. That afforded him the opportunity to study the people around him, watch their movements and know when danger knocked.

He left the house some minutes past 8 O'clock and began walking towards the direction of the sea. He slowed down his pace when he got close to the trash dump. He never wanted to be too early in any of his appointments. That was always suspicious and amateurish.

Straggling creepers covered both sides of the road and in the distance, the trash cans piled very high. The road was virtually deserted thus when he got to the dump, he had the place to himself. He looked at h5 wrist watch. It was 8.46 a.m. He went to the nearby bush and pretended to be urinating, while his eyes darted on either side off the bush and around the dump. He thought he heard a soft scratching noise, but couldn't be sure.

He came out of the road again and began to walk along the whole length of the dump which was piled so high that the cans and rusty tins on the apex had spilt down the road. He trod on the cans and continued. He came to an abrupt standstill when he saw a man squatting on a pile of cans smoking a cigarette. A car was parked farther down the road. He could see a man behind the wheel.

Nothing was said about a car and a second man, he speculated, but that did not mean that they would not be there. He looked closely at the man who stood up when he saw him and nodded. His description matched the one given him the previous day.

"The sun will shine very bright today," the man said. And the sea will be very still," he concluded.

"Have you seen the eagles?" Ageta asked. The man nodded. He reached down behind the pile of cans and his hand came out with a brown parcel done very neatly. Ageta came forward to collect the parcel. As his hand closed over it, a gun lumped into the man's hand, its barrel pointing at Ageta's stomach. He uttered an oath, his hand jerking away from the parcel. He took a step backwards.

"What is this?" he managed to ask.

"You have been betrayed to your enemies," the man said casually. "The consortium will look after you.

His fingers curled around the trigger. He squeezed gently. The silencer gun made a dull clap. The bullet hit Ageta on the chest. Another smashed his forehead. The third tore a neat hole in his heart. He slumped to the ground, scrabbling at the sandy surface. The man paused long enough to make sure that he was dead. He collected the parcel and ran to the car. The engine roared and tore out of the lonely patch of ground towards the sea.

* * *

Joe Lucas learnt about Ageta's death later that day when he finally located his tobacconist's shop and a kind neighbour had taken him to Ageta's shabby tenement quarters. He dashed off immediately and boarded the next available train to Washington. There he discovered that Bardi Orlando had disappeared. The frightened drugs man left town without any forwarding address.

Lucas was worried because he knew that Orlando betrayed Ageta. For a frightened man to do that, and leave behind a very successful business meant that those people played for high stakes alright. That lead was now permanently closed. He only had Simons' bugged telephone and the near cryptic remark about the First American Bank Shares to go along with. He hoped that they wouldn't prove to be blind leads like the present one.

Chapter Fourteen

They met in one of Paris' newer night clubs. The night was warm and humid and the sky was lit with a galaxy of stars. In the distance, the seine glittered with the wash of innumerable lights over its almost still surface. The skyline of Paris was as beautiful and as enchanting as ever, the Palace Elysee, a barely visible superb architectural design in the background.

A crowd, made up of mostly young people, milled in front of the night club from where a throbbing disco music issued. Taxis flashed past, some stopping to deposit more people in front of the nightclub.

The nightclub catered essentially for the young and they came dressed for the party. Most of them were clad in jeans and T-shirts, but quite an appreciable number of the girls wore either tight-fitting skin-coloured pants or minis. The front of the nightclub was neon-plastered and from the swing door entrance, there was the constant movement of people in and out of its exotic interior.

Joe Lucas and Lerec came dressed for the party. Masters of the chameleon life style, they knew that they had to adapt totally and subtly to the environment. Lucas wore a black jeans with stripes of red cloth material hanging out like tassels in several places. He had on a canvas shoe and a large blue T-shirt. His hair was close cropped and a dash of make-up here and there had restored the faded youthfulness in his face. Lerec wore a curdroy trousers and a check windcheater. He wore a punky wig designed in the latest hair style. He had a sneakers on his feet. Lucas had insisted on meeting the Frenchman in his territory, an idea Lerec, who avoided long distance travel if he could help it, welcomed. After much thought, he had hit on the idea of the night club and had advised Lucas to come dressed for the party.

The night club had been staked out for four nights running now by two of Lerec's special agents. Its mannerisms and other characteristics had been scrutinised and noted, and passed on to the two men. Even now, there were over ten special agents inside and outside the building, who blended with the surging crowd and kept a sharp lookout for any strange or unusual behaviour.

The two men were seated at a corner table in the dimly lit rectangular room. Their table and chairs were placed in such a way that they could easily observe those around them and all the movements at the swing door. The night club was full. Beyond the large dance floor was a raised platform where a mixture of bright and subdued lights played on three strip tease dancers. On the far right side of the platform was the discotheque, operated by shadowy figures who wore headphones. The bar was on the other side of the hall, away from the dance floor and close to a couple of doors that led down to the basement area where games of poker and slot-machines went on.

"Welcome to Paris," Lerec murmured to Lucas as they sipped their drinks. They had refrained from talking till one of the waitresses clad in bikini and a bra from which her large nipples stuck out, had served them and gone away. They barely heard the uproar around them.

"Paris is always a second home to me," Lucas replied.

"We have no time to waste," Lerec resumed. Things are moving at an extra-ordinary pace. I will give you the facts available to me so that we can compare notes when I hear what you have to say." He paused and took a sip at his drink. One of his hands was on the table, while the other one was propped up on his chin. Lucas said nothing. He looked at nothing in particular, but his mind was alert, taking in everything the Frenchman was saying.

"These are the things we already know - that is, the commission set up by the European Union Ministers of National Security. One is that there is a new, global drugs cartel that is intent on expanding the drugs trade, and as a prelude to that, the setting up of a powerful political and military machine that will take over the governments of countries strategic to their design. An American may be the head of that body. Two, is that large quantities of arms have already been purchased and a standing army is being built. Three is that powerful members of various governments are either willingly or unknowingly collaborating with those people. Four, is that our covers have already been blown as a result of the betrayal by those who happen to be where vital anti-drugs decisions are being made."

Lerec recounted the incidents at the Marseilles and the Rue d' Quassy and the fact that his own sources indicated that he, Lucas, had troubles of his own. Lucas smiled at that. "I'm closing in on the trailer in my own government. In the next couple of days, I will know who has been talking and why. But I will not make a move yet; I'll lead the fellow on till he or she leads up to the opposition." He took a sip again and glanced at the people dancing around them.

"We just got a break a couple of hours back. My contact at the Rue d' Quassy was only able to utter the name "Guttfri..." before he was gunned down. But he gave me sufficient background information about the man before he died. He had been digging quietly ever since and we may now have the first real name and face of one top-ranking member of this cartel. He is Guttfried Von Guttingberg, a small-time drugs dealer in the late 60s and 70s who suddenly disappeared. He may now be one of the operational chiefs of this organisation. He is constantly on the move but does not know that we are already on to him. We'll have something concrete in the next few days, unless you will rather want to participate in the hunt. So, what do you have for me?"

"Nothing that you don't already have an idea about," Lucas began. "My government has set out its own special team for this purpose, under the headship of a questionable character who may actually be the ears and eyes of this organisation in Washington. I'll be able to confirm this once I get back to the States. Two, is that they may have infiltrated a number of financial institutions in my country, not least being the First American Bank Shares. I have a number of leads there and will get back to you when something concrete gets out. I've also dispatched a number of agents to Colombia, Peru and Bolivia and will have their reports in a few days' time. I would have liked to be of help in the hunt for Guttingberg but the showdown with Simons is imminent. He is too near the White House for my comfort and if I could expose him, it will be sufficient embarrassment to the cartel. It may even throw them out of their stride, relying as they do, on the information he may have been passing on. We also have our theory about the leader of the cartel and are working steadily to unmask him."

So what do we do now?" Lerec asked. "Continue with our routine work. That is the name of our game. Get the name of the French traitor and capture our good friend Guttingberg. That will do from your side for now. For my part, if I could expose Simons, unravel the mystery at the First Bank Shares and get a lead on either the leader of this cartel or his South American associates, we could burst this thing wide open in two weeks or so." One other thing is that you should appoint a liaison officer between Paris and Washington. I don't think it's very healthy our being seen together. We can always set a time-table and let the liaison officer do the rest."

"That will be fine. You will hear from him in a matter of days." Lerec thought for a while. "The code name is "Windblows." He will describe the action of a tropical sand dune to you; especially sand dune in a desert clime. The antics of the adversary are not very different from the rage of a desert sand dune."

Lucas grinned at this bizarre comparison and looked at the Frenchman with deeper respect. He had heard a lot about him, and now that he had met him, he was not in the least disappointed. The name not only was a true professional, he also had a fertile imagination. The code name, 'windblows' was perfect for their purpose, for only the wind could scatter the gathering dunes to far and unwelcome places. Only windblows could flatten the desert sand dune to the level of nothingness. He grinned again.

Music blared around them and the dancers sweated out their hearts to the beat of the pop. Applause came after applause as the strip-teasers did their act. Waitresses squealed as their buttocks and breasts were pinched by the tipsy patrons, as they moved from table to table talking orders.

Lucas left before Lerec, hardly glancing at him as he went. They didn't shake hands. Two special agents watched him leave. They became very alert and their hands were set on their weapons. Lerec left about ten minutes later but not before whispering something to the ears of a giggling dance hostess who patted her curls at him and gave him sign that she would be right there waiting for him. The two agents followed closely behind him, watching the people intently.

* * *

Jean Jacques D'Atmand had just finished placing an urgent call to Barbara Alumineza with his cordless scrambled telephone set. He sat in his pent house suite, brooding over the events of the past week. His face was well drawn and the wrinkles on his forehead were pronounced. It had been a week of intense activities and endless meetings.

'This drugs business is maddening,' he reasoned. He had wanted an efficient agent to represent France in the European Union Special Commission and had picked Frelec. Now, he was bothered about the man's sheer capacity for work. He was turning in mass of security details and information that he had been unable to digest. More will still come tomorrow.

He glanced at his bulky briefcase with trepidation and frowned at the closely typed documents in them that awaited his attention. He remembered that he will be flying to Brussels in a week's time for yet another top priority briefing. After that will be the Rome Conference during which they will evaluate progress so far made. However, he knew that the Brussels and Rome trips will be disastrous unless he unwound. There was no better therapy for self-stimulation and rest than a couple of days with the provocative and irrepressible Barbara Alumineza.

Her voice had been very husky and romantic on the line. She had crooned his face and whispered about how much she adored him. He had hung up on her when she began her "dirty" talk. That would be a damned pretty waste, he reasoned, a waste he could ill afford at his age. Barbara would be with him, latest that night or the following morning. His nerves tingled at the thought.

He got up from the deep sofa on which he sprawled and plodded to the bathroom to take a shower preparatory to his mid-morning rest.

* * *

Generals Karl Kutz and Thong Wongo said very little throughout the duration of the Delta Airlines flight from Bangkok to Bogota. There was very little they would say because the time for talking had not yet come. They knew the calibre of man General Dos Santus was and felt better thinking deeply about what they had to say when they meet him. One had to be fully prepared before meeting with the mercurial and temperamental warlord if one had to get along with him. Kutz and Wongo wanted, more than anything else, to get along with their Commander-in-Chief. Both were happy with their appointments and wanted to protect their positions at all costs.

The journey had been very convenient, having come at the time Kutz was visiting the Golden Triangle on the invitation of Wango's boss - the message came just the previous day and they wasted no time in answering the summons of the council through General Dos Santus.

They reclined further back on their seats and closed their eyes to the persistent droning of the jet engines.

Chapter Fifteen

The man in military fatigues peered down through a pair of powerful binoculars at the woods around him. Beyond the oak trees and the creeping climbers the sea lay still, awash with the soft glow of the evening sun. He was well protected by the huge branches of the tree on which he sat astride two forked branches. He wore a blue beret and his feet was cased in tough riding boots. He swung the binoculars in the opposite direction and focused on a particular tree. He could barely make out another man who had a binoculars like himself and was also absorbed in his work. His constant scanning revealed six other men atop huge trees who kept steady watch over the dense woods.

Below on the ground, guards patrolled in Paris, their boots making soft sounds on the leave-stream ground, with their dogs on the leash. It was in the wooded region of the Scandinavian mountain and the mountain breeze was a welcome tonic to the men's hard work.

A track led off in the woods and terminated at a wooden building that lay covered by the thick woods. The wooden house had three rooms, a huge sitting-room, a bedroom with in-built toilet facilities and the other room that served as a kitchen. From one of the windows of the sitting-room, one had an uninterrupted view of the sea and could arouse himself with watching the occasional fishermen at work or the few ships and barges that navigated that part of the isolated sea. Neither the sailors nor the fishermen were aware of the existence of the wooden building and the occasional poachers were always turned away by the sign indicating that the land was private property which was protected by mined fences. No one had dared go near the mined fences; so no one had been injured by the mines.

It was an ideal place for a meeting, especially the kind that was now taking place inside the sitting-room of the wooden building. Jack Edmonds was as usual presiding, and the only member of the Council not present was Barbara Alumineza who was still with the French Minister of National Security, It was such a crucial meeting that they decided not to wait till she got back. It was decided that Edmonds should brief her about their decisions and get from her whatever information she might have from the minister.

From the empty coffee cups and the half-filled glasses on the table, it was obvious that the meeting had been in progress for quite sometime now. Edmonds cleared his throat and began to speak. He was at the head of a long table and was flanked on either side by the men and women of the consortium.

"Ladies and gentlemen," he said, "we've heard it all.
There is no time to waste. These are the things we must do now without delay. The American Joe Lucas and the Frenchman Frelec are both expendable. They must be eliminated. We have failed before in that direction; we cannot afford to fail again. We will place a stake on the head of Anthony Roberts of the First American Bank Shares."

He looked at some documents in front of him and suddenly looked at Guttfried. Von Guttingberg. "We can never be quite sure what the Frenchman Frelec will do with the scrap of information he got about you. But to be on the safe side, you have to go underground. And in doing that, you have to relinquish your political authority to Friedreich D'Atmec."

There was a murmur of approval from the assembly. Guttingberg bowed but said nothing.

"We will decide where and when you have to take a powder." Edmonds picked up a file folder and tapped on it. There was a sudden animated glitter in his eyes. The others knew what that folder contained having studied it for a long time now and having spent over two hours discussing it.

This is our operational package, the sum total of our military blueprint. I quite agree with the reasoning of the military commission and the high command. Special thanks should be given to Guttfried, General Dos Santus and their subordinates. Colombia will be the first to be taken. This will be followed by Bolivia and the Island of Belize. Our Asian operations will start from Khazakastan and move to Thailand and Malaysia.

We leave Europe and America as the last. I will personally

supervise that operation." There was silence in the room. Not a few hearts pounded because their hour of destiny was at hand and the day on which they will inherit the earth, near. They were all gripped with exhilaration along with a certain feeling of foreboding.

"There is one little matter we must settle once for all," he said. "And that will be for the benefit of Eric Donne, our expert on the African-American operations. Africa will remain outside our region of operations for now. It is a mere distraction, an unnecessary diversion. May be, in future when we would have re-ordered the world according to our new ethics, we will reckon with the existence of Africa. For now, any money, energy or resources poured in there will be a very big waste. Ladies and gentlemen, the meeting is closed.

* * *

Frelec surveyed the despatch in front of him and grinned at nothing in particular. His patience and perseverance had paid off finally. In front of him was the information he needed quickly about the whereabouts of the German, Guttfried Von Guttingberg. Though he moved constantly and was known to haunt most of the international hotels, resort centres and holiday spots the world over, he was known to keep a permanent home in a little village very near Munich. He got his information from his opposite number in Germany, who in turn got the information from a disillusioned drugs runner who felt by-passed in the last promotion exercise.

The man had sung his heart out, but nothing he said amounted to much that they did not already know except the information regarding Guttingberg's movement. The man was now under the protection of the German intelligence service and was guarded day and night.

Look-outs had been posted to the Munich residence of Guttingberg and they reported that he had left the house to watch it. He was expected back in four days' time.

This was the kind of information Frelec wanted; concrete data that he could work on. It was a refreshing change from the failure of the last month. He will not fail again, he promised him and reached for the glass of Perrier in front of him.

* * *

Joe Lucas also made significant progress in his. investigations. He had succeeded in tracking down a former staffer of the First American Bank Shares who was willing to talk for a prize. The man had left the establishment in a hurry, pleading failing health and the need to be closer to his family.

Lucas' enquiries showed otherwise. The man, Abrams, who was afraid of his shadow had taken to drinking to dull the constant fear of death that he knew was imminent. Lucas met him in a rundown tenement building in downtown Washington D.C. He had gone to waste, burying himself in his cheap whisky bottle virtually 24 hours of the day.

What the man had to say terrified Lucas and he was not a man to be terrified. Abrams revealed that First American was merely a conduit pipe for the movement of drugs money, and that through it very many banks and other financial institutions in America had become contaminated. Such monies amounted to hundreds of billions. He revealed that auto companies, computer firms, blue chip corporations and other industrial and service giants were funded by the drugs barons without the bulk of the management and share holders knowing the real sources of their buoyancy.

Abrams also told him that, going by the statistics he was exposed to and the movement of funds he had witnessed, over 30% of the entire USA high finance capital was related directly or indirectly to drugs money. Peter Nicholson, a murdered vice-president; was aware of this, and his death, Abrams said, was decreed by the powerful new drugs cartel. It was Nicholson's death that frightened and convinced him that his time was running out. Though he had made his move, he was still convinced that he was in grievous danger.

Lucas took a deep breath and posed the question that could make or mar the entire investigations. He looked at Abrarns' misty eyes, weak face and slack mouth asked:

"And who in your opinion has turned First American into this monster of the drugs barons? Who is the cartel's principal contact in that establishment?"

Abrams looked at him steadily for a moment. His hands trembled as he picked up his glass of raw whisky.

"Anthony Roberts," he said, "Anthony Roberts, the president of the Bank."

This information was astounding and Lucas knew that Roberts was so big that he could not be touched. Because he believed Abrams' story, he knew that the best approach was to organise a pinch and under disguise torture, if need be, for the information he wanted from Roberts. He had the men who would do it.

Of course, neither the agency nor Simons would know about this; it will be his own private operation.

Thinking about Simons, he wondered whether his bugging device had been detected. So far, nothing had come through. His relationship with Simons remained the same but they were both professionals. Even if Simons had detected and removed the bug and suspected that he planted it, he would never give himself away. The only good thing about it all was that it now gave him sufficient time to concentrate on the plans he had for Anthony Roberts. He would put that into effect before long; at least, not later than one week from the day he met Abrams.

* * *

Naku Chiba glanced at Tupa's preliminary report on his table and nodded. He had read the report a couple of times and was impressed by the man's professionalism and attention to detail. He knew that Tupa was the right man for the job he wanted; the present report lying in front of him convinced him that he thought right.

He was, of course, aware that a number of his key advisers, not least being the Minister of Internal Affairs, the Army Commander and the Inspector-General of police will oppose his plans with Tupa. But he will have his way in the end. He always did, using his superior intelligence and sheer force of logic to pacify his aides. They will come round to his way of thinking in the end. They always did. The only thing was that what he saw a year earlier, as clear as day light, only began to make sense to them eighteen months later. But that was why he was their leader, their guiding angel. He smiled at him and pressed the buzzer on his desk.

* * *

Jack Edmonds came out of the spacious bedroom in his Antigua hotel suite, wearing a huge green bathrobe and whistling to himself. His eyes took on an animated hue when he saw the gorgeous blonde on the double-bed. Her hair formed a halo beneath her head. She had a cigarette in her scarlet hand and was flipping through a literature. She was naked except for the portion of her left thigh and breast that was covered by the bed clothes.

* * *

She smiled at him. As he walked to the bed to join her, the telephone rang. He paused in his stride and reached for the receiver.

"An international call, Mr Edmonds," the operator said respectfully. "Put the person through," he replied. There were clicks on the line. Then Barbara Aluminiza's voice issued forth.

"The wind blows hot and furious over here," she said. "Germany has been hit by the first blast. They know about Munich, everything about Munich."

"Thank you," he said and replaced the receiver. He picked his cellular phone, punched some buttons and went inside the bathroom.

'Falcon,' he whispered. "Get all the Eagles ready. Munich has been touched. Repeat Munich has been touched. The contract sum is $100,000. Immediately." He came out of the bathroom looking pensive, his desire for the blonde quite forgotten.

Chapter Sixteen

The Berlin-Frankfurt Express train came to a stop in front of Frankfurt's main railway station. The engine croaked for a while and came to a final stop. The first class cabin doors swung open and passengers began to disembark.

There was the usual hustle and bustle typical of all rail stations. Porters carried suitcases and other goods on trolleys, closely followed by women and their children. The men clutched their suitcases and went in search of taxi cabs. There were ecstatic greetings by relations.

Guttfried Von Guttingberg came down from the first-class cabin cautiously. He surveyed the scene in front of him. He was alert. He was used to danger, but he had not experienced the feeling of apprehension which he felt now in all his violent, brutal adult life. He knew that danger was not far off; that those who were tracking him were still hot in pursuit, destroying the little freedom that he still enjoyed.

He never resented the commission's decision for him to go underground and relinquish his command of the political committee. He had been well provided for and knew that he would lack nothing in his whole period of isolation. He would be low for a while till the heat was reduced or his hunters got tired of looking for him.

But he had made it clear to Jack Edmonds that he would head back to Munich to pick a few vital things before taking off for one of the obscure Caribbean islands. He had also insisted that D'Armel's appointment should be in an acting capacity as he intended to re-establish himself as the head of the political committee when he came out of the cooler. Both wishes had been readily granted.

As he stepped down the rail platform, he remembered the day he met the Frenchman Febrae. The fellow had been alright, but Guttingberg knew that he would sell his mother to the highest bidder if his own life was under threat. His betrayal had confirmed that.

He gripped his suitcase tightly, pulled his hat well down his brow and looked around him. He knew that a reception committee would be waiting to take him to his hotel room and to ensure that he was safe till he completed his Munich mission and left Germany. He set off at a brisk pace, his face focused ahead but with his eyes darting here and there. As if by magic, two men came close to him and began walking by his side. He saw that one of the men was short, fat and bulky; while the other was a leathery man of medium height.

"Good day, Mr Guttingberg," the lean-looking man said, still keeping pace with him. "We hope you had a nice trip." Guttingberg said nothing. "We got Avalanche's message yesterday. The sun was still shining when he phoned. He will set sail when the sea is calm which will be in two days' time."

Guttingberg nodded and smiled at the two men. The password has been given and received. The men were genuine.

"May I carry your case?" the fat man offered. Guttingberg let him. "This way please," the first man said, "a car is already waiting for us." Together, they walked down the narrow way that .led out of the station towards the street that lay on the immediate left side of the station.

A dark Sedan was parked well out of the road, under a tree shade. The three men got in. The driver kicked the car to a start and looked over his shoulder inquiringly.

"The Votz hotel," the lean man snapped, "and snap it up." The driver grunted and sent the car shooting down the heavy traffic. Fifteen minutes of fast driving brought them to a quieter part of Frankfurt. The driver veered off the main road and took a right turn. He drove down the narrow street and stopped in front of the hotel Votz, a four storey structure.

"Wait for us here," the lean man commanded. "We will be down in ten minutes." The driver grunted again and drove to the car park which already had a number of cars.

The three men walked into the hotel, pushing the wing doors as they went. Facing them was a small lobby. On the right of the lobby was the reception desk. They trooped in front of the reception desk. A man was behind the counter. "You have a reservation for Mr. Blane," the lean man said. It was a statement, not a question. The reception clerk looked up inquiringly and reached for his register. He thumbed open a few pages and ran down the names .on a particular page with his index finger. He looked up again. "Yes, master. We do have a reservation in that name."

"Let's have the room key, please," the lean man said again, "and be quick with the formalities." The clerk took down a key from a set behind him which were hanging on a peg and gave them to the man.

"Room 214; first floor fourth-room on the right, as you come out of the lift."

"Save your breath," the man said again. "We will not get lost." The written formalities over, the three men got into the lift.

"Room 214 was a double room, simply furnished but decent. The fat man dumped the suitcase on the bed and moved to the window. He glanced behind him and drew the curtain close. Guttingberg was flipping through some papers on the desk when he felt a tap on his shoulder. He swung around and gave a sharp gasp when he saw the long barrel of a silencer pistol pointing at him.

"This is where you get yours," the lean man said. The fat man had his gun out too.

"What is this?" Guttingberg managed to ask. "Avalanche phoned Falcon who instructed us about what to do. Your cover has been blown wide open. German and French security agents are already waiting in your Munich home. You know too much Mr Guttingberg. Would you allow the Consortium to fail because of what you know. That won't be fair." The man spoke rapidly, taking a step or two back as he spoke.

"Wait a minute," Guttingberg said. "A mistake must have been made." "No mistake has been made. The information came through a couple of hours ago. Your guards have been charged. We are to see that you do not talk. Good bye Mr Guttingberg." The lean man's hand closed over the trigger. He squeezed it gently. The bullet made a dull noise as it imbedded itself inside Guttingberg's chest. Another bullet smashed his wind pipe. Yet, the third nearly tore his neck off his head. He fell violently forward, his questing hand reaching for nothing. The two men shoved their weapons inside their jacket pockets, dragged his body to the bathroom and emptied the content of his briefcase. They took away a couple of papers which they tipped off the case's false button, gave one more passing glance at the inert body and went out of the room fast.

* * *

"Pull up here," the lean man directed the driver when he saw a public telephone booth. The car came to a halt on the grassy curb. The lean man got out of the car and went to the booth. He slotted some coins and began to dial.

"Eagle to Falcon; Eagle to Falcon," he whispered. He paused for a moment and then spoke rapidly.

"Avalanche's orders have been carried out, Falcon. Eagle has done his own part. I will expect the shipment in four days, same place, same account." He left the booth and got inside the car. The car pulled off the curb into the steady stream of traffic.

* * *

The voice on the other side of the line was muffled as if the caller was speaking with a handkerchief draped over the receiver. Frelec strained his ears to catch what the muffled, scratchy voice was saying. It was late evening and he was in his office, monitoring the progress of the hunt for Guttingberg.

"Pardon me Mr., what was it you were saying?" he apologised.

"Do not ask me who i am or where I am calling from," the voice said, "because I won't tell you. Do not even attempt to trace this call. That will be futile. Just listen to what I am saying."

"Go on, please," Frelec said patiently. The caller must be a practical joker, but in his profession, Frelec had learnt to give every man his due.

"The search for Mr Guttingberg is unfortunately over. You have lost again. Get in touch with your German partners. Let them send somebody to the Hotel Votz in Frankfurt. Guttingberg must be somewhere there, very dead. Good luck Mr Guttingberg."

"Wait a moment," Frelec almost shouted. "You said that Mr Guttingberg must be in...." He discovered that he was talking to himself. He listened for a moment to the continuous droning sound of the receiver and dropped it on its cradle. Frelec was not easily rattled, having faced so many dangerous situations in his career as a secret agent. But he was rattled now.

He picked up the receiver again and dialled a German number. "Yes Johannes, a call just came in now - must be a joker. No, not here. But in Frankfurt. Yes, he said the Hotel Votz. Please do a quick check for me. Do you say, two hours? Okay, I will wait." He dropped the receiver, relaxed back in his chair and prepared for the two hours' wait.

Two and half hours later, the telephone rang. He jumped out of his chair and picked the receiver. "Is that you Johannes? Okay, shoot." He clutched the receiver to his ears, hardly believing what he was being told.

"We are sorry, Mr Frelec," the voice at the other end said. "We have made a thorough check. It's Guttingberg alright. The description in the photograph matched. There was also a message. It reads: 'We shall be right there at the end; we will be waiting for all the foes of progress till the end of times.' It was written with Guttingberg's blood. Well, we will try, but I bet you, they have left Germany by now. Yes, he got their description, but of what use will that be? Okay, we will keep you posted."

The connection was broken. Frelec glanced at the receiver in his hand dumbly and lowered it back on its cradle wearily. He had never felt deflated like this in his entire career. First, was the Marseilles thunder. Then the murder at the Rue d' Quassy. And now this. Who must be talking in Paris? Who has such powers to know everything that he knew such that he hit a blind alley before he even began to make his move? He held his head in his hands, unable to think.

* * *

Jack Edmonds removed the handkerchief from the mouthpiece of his handset and placed the handset on the table. There was an animated look in his eyes and there was glow in his face. He looked younger and felt very confident in himself and his abilities. He was not given to this kind of exhibitionism or display of pride, thinking them to be a mere waste of time but he could not resist talking to the Frenchman, Frelec.

He was annoyed that they still dared him and the interest he represented and he wanted them to know the extent of his powers. He felt sorry for Guttingberg, for he had liked the burly German very much but the interest of the consortium far outweighed the life of an individual.

As he went to bed that night, he reflected that in a couple of weeks' time, they will be in control of at least, three Asian and three South American countries.

After them, it will be the turn of Europe and America. Such thoughts soothed his nerves; they made him sleep well.

Chapter Seventeen

They had been waiting in the shadows for the past one and half hours. The vacant lot was overgrown with tall grasses and afforded the men the cover they needed. Through the opening they made in the grass they could see the entrance to Anthony Roberts' house. The front of the house was in deep shadow, as was the rest of the house, except for one of the upper floor windows. There were four of them, highly dangerous and well-trained men who carried out their assignments with professional efficiency.

Joe Lucas waited with one other man on the thick hedge opposite the house. A narrow road separated the hedge from the house. He knew that Roberts was in town because one of his men had placed an innocuous call to the office earlier in the day. But they had not seen him when they got to the neighbourhood a little over 7 pm. They had met the house in near total darkness. They knew that he would not be in because the look-out man had phoned that Roberts drove out about 6.30 pm. He went away alone. Lucas only prayed that he came back alone. He wanted to avoid violence as much as possible.

All his men were trained to wait, so they all waited patiently. A few minutes after 9 pm, they heard the sound of a car driving down the quiet, almost unused street. The men came on the alert. They all knew what to do. The headlights of a car pierced the darkness and the car came to a leisurely stop in front of the house. They had decided to make the pinch when he was about driving off.

Lucas was relieved to see that Roberts came back atone. He nodded with satisfaction. Roberts drove to the back of the house where the garage was. The men waited, praying that he never decided to use the back entrance. There was stillness everywhere except for the gentle rustling of the grasses as they were caressed by the wind.

As a shadowy figure came round the back of the house to the entrance, the silence of the night was again shattered by the sound of a heavy car. The car screeched to a halt in front of the house, its rearlight lighting up the road and the immediate vicinity of the compound. Three men dashed out of it and walked towards Roberts who stood rooted on a spot. They had all drawn their guns and walked with a steady crouch.

Lucas racked his brain about what to do. He knew what he would do, but could not say what his men would do. He hoped that their training could stand them in good stead now. He knew who the men were; or more correctly who sent them. The leaders of the cartel must have decided that Roberts knew too much and was becoming dangerous. These must be paid killers sent to silence him.

Without hesitation, he pulled out his pistol, took an aim and fired. One of the men dropped to the ground, yelping in pain. His immediate companion also took an aim and fired. The second man clutched his throat, took a stumbling run and fell heavily on the ground. The third man whirled round and began to fire blindly at the direction of the two shots. He made a perfect target for the other four men. Three of them fired simultaneously while the fourth dashed forward and made a grab for Roberts.

The engine of the assassins' car roared loudly. The driver put the car on reverse and began driving desperately down the road. Lucas steadied his aim and took a snap shot at the disappearing car. He heard the sound of shattering glasses. The car reversed at the next intersection and roared away on a violent change of gear.

The men had now caught hold of Roberts and hauled him into their get way car. He was quivering like a reed being blown by a violent wind. Lucas, who wore a black mask got in the back with Roberts. Another man joined the driver in front. The rest entered the second car. As their engines revived and the drivers engaged their gears, they could hear the violent barking of dogs, and in the far distance, the sound of approaching police sirens. They took the other side of the road, away from the direction the driver of the cartel's car went.

* * *

The cellar was unlit except for a 60-watts naked bulb that hung from the ceiling. Anthony Roberts was strapped to an iron chair in the middle of the room. His hands and legs were bound with tough copper wire. This too was wound round his body and the iron chair.

He blinked at the harsh light of the bulb and looked at the masked man in front of him. He was very frightened and his bowel threatened to give up. There was a bitter taste in his mouth; the taste of one who was very sick. The masked man did not trouble him. It was rather the two others in the room that held his morbid attention. They were shirtless. Their muscles ripped as they moved their hands. Sweat glistened down their broad, hairy chests. They both had brutal, scarred faces that were moronic in their vile expressionlessness.

Joe Lucas spoke behind his mask. He was in no particular hurry with the interrogation. "Good evening, Mr Roberts," he said mood English. "I'm sorry to put you through this inconvenience." Roberts was not impressed by the man's polished accent or his refined manners. If he meant well for him, what will those two brutal goons be doing in the room, he thought.

"Count yourself a very lucky man," Lucas continued. "You would have been very dead had we not come at the time we did. We know who the men are, as you do, so we can skip that part. I have a question for you and I want your detailed answer to it. Do not hesitate, do not lie, do not try to be brave. You will talk in the end. These two fellows over here are angry with me for treating you like a gentleman. I do not want to annoy them further. Answer my question and you will be home in less than one hour. If you decide to be stubborn, well...." He left the sentence hanging.

Anthony Roberts was no hero. He was just an ordinary banker. He knew that it will get him nowhere being difficult. He made up his mind that he will tell this gentle thug all he knew, provided that he had the answer to his question.

"What do you want from me?" he managed to ask.

"That is good," Lucas replied. "Listen carefully, I will not repeat my question. Tell me all you know about the role of your bank and yourself in the new global drugs business, the methods employed by the drugs barons in their money laundering business, the institutions and agency where this money is passed to and the leaders of the new global drugs cartel?"

Roberts swallowed a lump that came to his throat. A fourth man had entered the room carrying a tape recorder and a chair. He placed the chair behind Lucas and handed him the tape recorder. Lucas sat on the chair and switched on the recorder.

Roberts took a deep breath, looked around him like a trapped animal. When one of the men made a threatening move, Lucas waved him back to his position.

"I will tell you all I know mister, all I know, honest to God. I just want to go home." "That's fine, shoot." Roberts began to talk.

* * *

Escravor Odaja was in a Bogotan night club when the message came to him. He was having a swell time with his companions comprising three female and two male. They were all gaudily dressed. Several of his bodyguards had made themselves very comfortable in the club, either sipping drinks or watching the sex dancers. Others were strategically located outside, indistinct in their attires and very much part of the background of the crowded downtown neighbourriood. There were three escort cars stationed at a distance of fifty meters from one another. One was very close to the entrance of the night club. The other was a little distant on the right. The third was on the left.

Odaga liked to travel like a real baron. An extravagant man, he enjoyed all the trappings his trade brought in to the full and was not modest with his wealth. He had a house in his native Peru, a mansion in New York City, a castle in the remote mountains of Medellin and a beach home in Belize.

Though it was the responsibility of Jack Edmonds to issue the directive on all hired killings, it was Odaga who saw to the implementation of such directives. He was the head of the consortium's murder Inc. Committee, not that it went by that blatant title. It was rather called committee on External Conflict Resolution. While Edmonds, the Avalanche was the soul of an operation, it was Odaga, the Falcon who executed the deed.

Resplendent in his white tuxedo, with matching chains, rings and bracelets, he was least prepared for the news that came to him.

He rarely failed in any contract he commissioned as the case of Guttingberg had recently demonstrated. So, he was not in the least bothered about the task of eliminating Anthony Roberts. To him, Roberts was a dead man the moment the pronouncement was made. He had responded quickly to Avalanche's directive and was set to receive the good news anytime thereafter.

Two men appeared at the door, weaving their way in and out of the surging crowd. Some of his bodyguards stiffened when they saw the new entrants but relaxed on recognizing at least one of them. The men made their way to Odaga's table and paused at a respectable distance. He barely glanced at them, engrossed as he was with his animated conversation with one of the ladies whose transparent dress and fair-sized breast that jutted out impressively was very distracting.

Odaga paused in the steady flow of words that issued out of his mouth and beckoned on one of the men. The man came close, bent low by the side of his chair and began to give him the briefing.

"A report just came in Sir," he said. "The operation was a failure. There was a reception committee waiting at the house. Three of our men were killed. The driver escaped. But he stayed long enough to see that the banker was kidnapped, not killed. One of the men wore a mask. We suspect that he is the American Lucas." Rage discoloured Odaga's face. His eyes turned dusky red. The man took a step back, but still maintained his semi-crouching position.

"Get out," Odaga said harshly. "Both of you. Tell the boys to get ready. I'll be out in five minutes."

The two men walked out of the night club, treading the ground as if it was made of egg-shells. A few minutes later, Odaga stood up and beckoned on his companions. The party walked out of the night club. Once he was inside his limousine, Odaga slipped his cellular phone out of his jacket pocket, punched some buttons and waited.

"Falcon to Avalanche. I am coming in. The quarry was spirited off. The shipment could not get through. I fear the bird is already singing. What shall the sailors do?" He listened for a further three minutes, punched another button and put the handset back inside his jacket. He turned to the driver and said simply: "Step on it, I have an appointment to meet at Palace Hotel." The car roared along the busy highway.

Chapter Eighteen

BIeep, bleep, bleep. Joe Lucas gave a start and jumped up from the bed. He reached inside his coat pocket and zipped down the carefully concealed opening that housed the bugging device. It was a few hours after he had listened to Anthony Robert's confession and he was worn out.

He had made a few telephone calls and visited his friend, Jonas who had confirmed some of the assumptions he had after talking to Roberts. His meeting had been quite fruitful. He got home late, thoroughly tired, and worn out. It had been a hectic day but he was happy that he almost achieved the impossible. He now had a vague idea of the leader of the new cartel and he was more than convinced about Simons' complicity in the whole plot.

He had decided to stretch himself out on the bed for a short while before deciding on the next line of action. He had almost dozed off before he heard the distinct bleep from the bugging machine, a machine he had almost decided was now worthless. He picked up the machine and quickly touched a knob on its flat side. A deep blue light glowed off and on. He pressed the machine to his ear and began to listen, his heart beating faster than normal.

The conversation came clearly to him. Simons was filching with somebody he called Avalanche.

Avalanche: "The wind has been blowing hot lately. First Shares may have talked. The grass is no longer safe because the wind has flattened the reeds."

Simons: "What is the grass to do? Will the grass flee before the wind or should it go under ground?"

Lucas could detect the thinly veiled panic in Simons' voice. He could also hear the pounding of his heart. There was a praise on the other line.

Simons: "Avalanche, Avalanche, are you still there?"

Avalanche: "I have been thinking. Its time for the grass to move. The pacific has been quiet of late. The water is still and the breeze of the coast fans the sleepy Islands all around. You will be met at the Florida Coast. Miami is the spot we desire. Three eagles will approach you at the lobby of the Hilton at precisely 17.30 p.m. Three days from now."

Simons: "The grass will keep the date. The grass will avoid the blaze till then. I'll be prepared and I will be waiting at the Hilton."

Avalanche: "Together we will conquer the elements, together we will build the new dunes."

Simons: "Together, good old Avalanche, together. Send my love to Falcon."

The connection was broken. Lucas replaced the machine in its hidden recess after pressing again on the knob. So, Simons was about to skip. The man called Avalanche, presumably the cartel leader he has been stalking, had alerted him about the Roberts kidnap and warned him that his cover may have been or will be blown soon. Arrangements had been made to sprint him out of the USA to one of the obscure Pacific Islands. Simons will meet with the agents of the cartel at the lobby of the Hilton Hotel in Miami from where he will be flown in a chartered plane to his new home. Well, Lucas thought, it will be quite a meeting. Not only will there be agents of the new anti-drugs agency, the CIA and the FBI also waiting, he himself will personally lead the operation against a man whose warped sense of value and greed was capable of destroying his country and the security of mankind.

He removed the bug from his pocket again and looked at it intently and admiringly. He walked to the inner room that served as a bathroom, toilet and store. He pulled open a carefully concealed panel and reached for a button in its dark recess. The door sprang open. He took out a small box that was inside a thick carton. This he took to his sitting-room cum bedroom. He laid the box on the table. He pressed another button on the side of the box after removing the carton and the steel box snapped open. Inside was a very sensitive tape recorder with an external flat shaped extender. He brought out a cassette tape from one of the drawers in the cabinet near the window and slotted it in. He then fixed the bugging machine to the flat-shaped extender and pressed the play and record buttons.

* * *

It was pure routine in the office the following morning as far as Joe Lucas was concerned. He greeted the other staffers warmly and made his way to Simons' office at the far end of the building. Though Simons managed a charming smile and gripped his hand warmly, Lucas could detect traces of intense stress on his boss' face. The wrinkles on his forehead were more pronounced than ever and the lines on his mouth were deep and clearly etched. He looked worried but tried bravely to cover it by an uncharacteristic bustleness.

"Lest I forget, Joe," he addressed Lucas." A report just came in. Its about a slaying in Bogota a few days' back. Looks as if somebody got talking. He must have talked out of turn. His body was riddled with bullets. His identity, his suspected killers - who obviously are working for this cartel - are all here." He tapped on a flat file that was lying on the top of his desk.

"I guess I will study it right away. Have you gotten further contact from your opposite number in France?" he asked.

"Not yet, except that your pal, Lerec, is busy digging for the source of the dangerous leaks that have embarrassed them of late. He hopes to have something tangible in a few days. He agreed to let us have the details the moment he strikes something positive."

Sirnons gave him the file. "I will be in the office till 1 p.m." Lucas said. "My report on this case will be ready then. I have a contact to meet between 2 and 6 p.m. I will be back to the office briefly by 7 p.m. and go home by 8.30 p.m. In case you want to reach me after 9 p.m I will be meeting another contact at Lucky's Inn in 162nd Avenue between 8 and 12 mid-night."

Simons nodded. Though Lucas was watching his face carefully, the trained professional kept his face very bland.

Lucas spent a couple of hours in his office going over routine matters, including the worthless file that Simons gave him. At precisely 1 p.m. he locked his office, walked to the curb and halted a taxi. "Keep moving," he told the cab man. "I will tell you where I will be going in a short while."

The driver engaged the gear and sent the car shooting down the busy highway. Lucas glanced back but saw no other car take off after them. He relaxed in his seat but kept a sharp look out through the side mirror at the stream of traffic behind them.

The ride was a smooth one with no incident on the way. Lucas never expected to encounter the opposition in this particular journey. He knew the time to watch out was in the office in the evening and at Lucky's Inn later that night. He had deliberately dropped that information with Simons and would be surprised if he failed to set up a trap. He shrugged his shoulders, stepped out of the car and made his way to his destination, a distance of about one hundred meters down the road.

* * *

Simons glanced at his watch. The time was 1 .45 p.m. His heart was heating dully and there was a bitter taste in his mouth. He knew that only Lucas knew about his real identity and as a professional he will keep his secret to himself till he had made sure of his facts absolutely. He suspected that he still had over two days to plan things and considered the options open to him, If only Lucas knew his connection with the consortium and Lucas was eliminated, then all would still be well. But if he suspected that Lucas will alert others, then the best option would be to get out fast. If he had known that Lucas tapped his telephone he would have made a run for it. He still felt relatively safe to manoeuvre.

He got up from his desk and made his way to the outer office.

"Take all my urgent calls," he instructed his secretary. "I'll be back in half an hour. Tell Adams to wait for me if he comes in my absence."

He entered his car and drove down the road. At the next intersection, he turned right and drove down a narrow street. He stopped the car a short distance from a drugs store, cut the engine and walked the rest of the distance. He shut himself up in a nearby pay booth at the left side of the entrance of the store, dropped some coins into the hole and dialled a number with a slightly trembling hand.

"Grass to Avalanche," he whispered. There was a response at the other end of the line. "Listen carefully. One of the wind blowers will be in the office between 7 p.m. and 8.30 p.m. this evening, and at Lucky's Inn in 162nd Avenue between 9 p.m. and 12 midnight. Good hunting." He dropped the receiver back on its cradle, wiped his sweating face with a handkerchief and left the pay booth. He glanced at either side of the road, and nodding at nobody in particular went towards his car.

* * *

CIA director, Chris Williams, looked at Joe Lucas the way an acclaimed scientist would regard an unknown microbe. It was unusual for such a field officer to see the director on such a short notice but Lucas had played it smart. He had written his message in a sealed enveloped and given it to Williams' secretary to deliver to his boss. His message was very simple: he had information that not only threatened the job of the CIA director but the very survival of the USA. Williams must see him, now, or in two days' time he will cease to be the CIA director.

Williams frowned deeply when he read the message. If he had not known Lucas by reputation he would have had him arrested, but he regarded the field man very highly. He had approved his recruitment as the operational chief of the new anti-drugs agency. Then, he had smiled. The fellow knew that he didn't have a chance of seeing him in a week's time and had decided on this bravado approach. Well, he will see him, and he better not waste his time. He will be sorry, it he did.

"Such an insulting way to book an appointment," Williams said soberly. "What are you playing at?" His tone, however, was devoid of anger. When dealing with these twisted, and sometimes paranoiac agents, one had to be careful, he thought, recollecting a nasty experience a few years back when a highly rated agent suddenly went berserk during briefing and demonstrated his knowledge of mental arts on the company's analysts and psychotherapists.

"I hope your office is free of bugs," Lucas said, looking him straight in the face. He was sitting on a straight backed chair facing Williams.

"Is it as serious as that?"

"Yes."

"Shoot, everything is okay" Lucas took a deep breath. He had decided to come to Williams because of two reasons. One, he actually recommended Simons who had been a protegee for several years. Second, he was beyond reproach, so there was noway he could be working for the consortium. If such a man as the CIA director was working for the opposition, then he had even little choice, for it was akin to saying that the president was a Russian spy.

He took another deep breath. "Simons is the point man of drug consortium in the USA," he said quietly. Williams looked at him as if he had taken leave of his senses. But Lucas' grave look, the lines of worry on his face and the determined tilt of his chin warned Williams that the fellow was dead serious.

"What!" he exclaimed. "What are you talking about?"

"Exactly what I said. Simons is the link between our country and the new global drug consortium. I have the facts."

William's mouth hung open. His ball point slipped out of his hand; and he seemed as if he had difficulty in breathing. "Facts, you said?" he managed to gasp out. Let's have them.

"Sir, I will crave your indulgence to start from the beginning. When I was contacted for this assignment and was told that Simons will be in charge of the operation, I had my doubts but made counterplans. I have worked with him in two other operations and on each occasion an enemy agent had disappeared mysteriously from our station cell. They have never been seen till date. On each occasion, everything pointed to Simons' complicity. He had enunciated his idea of patriotism to one and the bottom line is that one must work for his country while at the same time taking care of himself. He didn't push it far; neither did he make it sound odious. But I noted them."

"Go on," Williams whispered.

"So I had my doubts about him. It's not just that he was not forthcoming on ideas on this case but that he deliberately suppressed vital information that could lead to any successful investigation. I have my facts on that. He sends agents on worthless wildgoose chase, and I will be surprised if you have been briefed on anything concrete since this operation began."

Williams arched his brows. He recalled his embarrassment by the president who wanted to know how far his team was progressing. He nodded his head slowly.

"I had his scrambled telephone bugged after unscrambling it," Lucas continued. "Through my other contacts and links I got to know about the involvement of the First American Bank Shares in the consortium's network and the murder of one of its vice-presidents. I set a trap for its president, under disguise, and have a sworn statement made by him. He has revealed the entire financial network of the narcotics industry in the USA and Simons' role in the entire operation. He has given me sufficient clue about the leader of this group, a highly respected citizen of this country, if my guess is right. My patience paid off well. Simons, code-named "Grass" talked with this man who goes by the code-name Avalanche. Avalanche warned Simons that his cover may have been blown and that they have plans to fly him to an obscure Caribbean Island, the day after tomorrow via Miami at 17.30 p.m. in the lobby of the Hilton Hotel. I have a transcript of their conversation here." He brought out the tape from his inner coat pocket, and laid it on the desk in front of Williams. The latter looked at it with fright and pushed it over to his side of the desk. Lucas didn't tell him that he had made a copy for himself, including his own narration about the operation. That copy was now lying in a safe deposit box.

"I saw him early this morning and told him that I will be working in the office between 7 and 8.30 p.m. and will be at a local bar called Lucky's Inn between 9 p.m. and 12 midnight. I am sure that he must have contacted his people by now. Send a couple of chaps to the vicinity of the office before seven and at Lucky's bar by 9 pm. I will set a trap for them."

Williams reached for a cassette player in one of his desks, brought it out and placed it on the desk. He slotted in the tape and began to listen to the clear conversation. When that was over, he removed the tape and put the player back inside the drawer. He then reached for one of the telephones on his desk. As his hand touched the receiver, Lucas moved quickly and placed his hand over Williams'

"What do you want to do, Sir?" he asked softly.

"Have him picked up and detained till I verify some of the details which are still unclear. No doubt he is our man, and there's no point in wasting time."

"That may be right, Sir," Lucas said, "but we'll not achieve anything from that. Simons will not talk. I even suspect he has a cyanide somewhere. He is of no use to us, but he could lead us to our objective. Today's rendezvous will give you all the proof you need. But, most importantly, we need him in Miami. We need him to lead us to the Avalanche. The show-down may be more imminent than we thought." He removed his hand from Williams', who in turn removed his from the receiver.

Thank you, Mr. Lucas," he said simply. "I agree with your reasoning. Arrange for the Miami meeting. We will all be there.

Chapter Nineteen

The Washington - Miami flight was smooth and pleasant. Everything was on schedule as it ought to be. In one of the seats in the business class a tall, bearded man with close cropped thinning hair reclined and was reading the morning papers. There was a deep scar running from his right eye to his jaw which the lush growth of hair barely covered. There was also an old scar on the corner of the left side of his mouth which caused it to droop down a little, giving him an aggressive look. A closer look would also reveal that the sole of one of his shoes was taller than the other, giving the indication that the man walked with a slight limp.

Joe Lucas' disguise was perfect and not even his mother would recognise him. The lead was not real. So was the scar on his face and at the corner of his eyes. His close cropped hair and the thinning temples were also the handiwork of a master cosmetician who was sworn into secrecy about the personality wearing the disguise. The additional inch to the left sole completed the transformation and Lucas was confident that he would walk past Simons without the latter giving him even a second glance.

As he placed the paper on the stool by his side and reached for his steaming cup of black coffee, Lucas thought with satisfaction about the events of the previous two days. The trap did not take place at the office because the place was well guarded. He had stayed in the office till 8.30 pm with five CIA agents hiding outside but nothing had happened. It was at Lucky's Inn that the hit was attempted. He never attempted to disguise himself providing, as he did, a perfect target for his assailants. The attempt was made as he was leaving the Inn about 12.30 a.m with three patrons who happened to be CIA agents. A command had been issued somewhere and Out of the gloom about four men came out shooting. The encounter was brief; the match unequal. Lucas and his partners had flattened themselves on the ground as the night was lit up with gun flashes. Shots came from several directions and before long it was all over. Three of the assailants were caught down by the over ten agents who had taken positions at different approaches to the Inn. One was seriously wounded and was now being guarded by CIA agents in an obscure but well-equipped hospital somewhere in Washington. He would be ready to talk in a couple of hours.

The following day had been the same at the office. Work was routine in the office.

Towards the close of work, Simons summoned Lucas and told him that he would be travelling to New York the following day. He would be expected back in two days' time. He had conveniently displayed his Washington - New York ticket for Lucas' benefit. Lucas wished him safe journey.

Lucas had confirmed that Simons left that evening for Miami with two luggages and a thick briefcase. He smiled as the agent stationed at the airport gave him the news. He decided to take the morning flight, in order to get to Miami on time, settle into the Hilton and wait at the lobby. He was travelling with six of the CIA and anti-drugs agency's special agents. Seven others had already travelled to Miami the previous day. Three in fact, who were recalled from overseas assignments, were on the same flight that took Simons to Miami. They were to brief him about Lucas' movements since touching down at the Florida Coast.

The skyline of tall palms, palmettoes, beaches and flashing buildings told Lucas that the journey was about to end. The touch down and taxiing on the runway were also smooth. The usual airport formalities over, Lucas was picked up in a cab that materialised out of nowhere, driven by one of the special agents. Lucas admired the sun bathers, the beach worshippers and the skimpily clad gorgeous girls that lined the sidewalks as the car took him to the Hilton which had a direct view to the ocean.

He checked into his room, unpacked and took his bath, being very careful with his make-up. He called room service and asked for fruit salad and a jug of water. Thereafter, he decided to take a nap before his briefing by the agents who had arrived the previous day. That he knew will still leave him with almost two hours to take a general stock of the situation at the lobby and plan on the best way to catch Simons in the act.

Lucas' briefing by two of the CIA special agents was carried out in an isolated part of the hotel garden. He learnt that Simons arrived the previous night and was received by three gentlemen in suit, two of who appeared to be European, and the third who was unmistakably Latino. He was driven off soon after his arrival without checking into any of the hotel rooms. All attempts to tail them, the agents revealed, failed because they switched cars a couple of times and had an escort of about three other cars with them.

Lucas also learnt that the agents could only guess about Simons' destination last night at only three kilometres' certainty. Simons, they also told him, never came back to the hotel that night nor was he seen throughout the day.

"Our problem now," one of the agents stated, "is whether he was alerted that he may be followed and if they have decided to change the location of their contact today."

"It's a chance we have to take," Lucas said, wondering whether all their elaborate preparations would come to nought. He thought otherwise. "It's usually the standard procedure in matters of this nature," he continued. "I still think that he would show up at the Hilton. Nevertheless, we have no other choice, except one. Meeting anytime from now between him and any of our men stationed within the general area you described; we cannot roam the whole of Miami looking for him."

"I guess that will be all," the other agent who had said nothing so far stated. We have to get back to the hotel in case they decide to shift the time for their rendezvous."

They walked back to the hotel as would three gentlemen who had just taken a look at the garden, and probably discussed business of mutual interest. At the lobby they separated, the two agents going towards the direction of the rich sofas, while Lucas heading for the lifts to get back to his room. He had a few more things to do, and a couple scrambled calls to make before the D-time. He wanted to be in the lobby about twenty minutes before Simons' arrival, if at all he will still show up - enough time to observe the general situation of the contact ground but not too long enough to attract any attention or suspicion.

At precisely 1 7.08, he left his room and headed for the lift once more. By 1 7.10, he was at the lobby area. He chose a seat that was so strategically placed as to afford him a view of the massive swing doors. He placed a couple of newspapers, his cigarette box and lighter on the low table in front of the chair, walked to the bar and ordered gin and tonic.

He got back to the chair, opened one of the papers and began to scan the headlines. He looked out of the corner of his eyes and saw a number of the CIA and FBI agents seated comfortably at different parts of the lobby, engaged in one uninteresting activity or the other. He nodded slowly, satisfied that all that needed to be done had been taken care of. Everything now depended on luck. He turned his gaze once more to the swing doors.

At 17.27 p.m. the doors swung open and a family came bustling in. There was the flattish man in straw hat and beach shirts; his wife in a gaudy outfit and three kids who kept a continuous prattle as they walked past where Lucas sat on their way to the lifts. At 1 7.28, barely a minute after the happy family had bustled past the doors swung open again and Simons was silhouetted at the door. Lucas' heart skipped a beat and then raced. He forced his racing heart to stop and continued with both his reading and watching Simons' movement. Simons looked this way and that way and entered the lobby almost reluctantly. He looked haggard and harassed and there were bags under his eyes as if he did not have enough sleep the previous night.

He made his way to the far side of the lobby very close to where one of the agents sat. They glanced at one another, and nodded their heads in casual acquaintance. The agent reached for his drinks as Simons sat on a vacant seat, swung around to face the battery of lifts at the other side of the lobby.

17.30 p.m. The lift came gently down and a couple of men and women stepped out. A few of them started walking towards the reception desk. Others made their way to the door. Three men started advancing towards Simons. They sat very close to him, making light conversation.

"Good evening, Mr. Thomas," one of them said, "welcome to the Hilton."

"Thank you," Simons replied. "I hope everything is on schedule."

"All our arrangements are perfect," the man said. "Mr. Jorges is waiting for you in his room. If you will care to follow us. You will be leaving in twenty minutes' time."

The four men stood up and walked back to the lift. The agent gave an elaborate yawn and followed them at a sedate pace. Lucas was already at the mouth of the lift and the five of them entered the cage. The lift stopped on the 10th floor. The men all stepped out as the door swung open gently. Simons and the three men walked to the door at the passage and paused at the door of room 1024. Lucas walked past the door, the other agent behind him. He turned slightly and in time to see the men enter the room. He was in one mind whether to make the snatch here but thought against it. Too much risk to be taken. Too much ground and distraction.

"Meet me at the lobby in eighteen minutes," he told the agents. Have all the cars ready." The agent turned and walked towards the lift. Lucas continued on his way down the long broad passage.

* * *

The night was very cool and breezy. They had been travelling for over ten minutes now. Lucas looked at the luminous dial of his strap-watch. The time was 1 8.29 p.m. Ahead of him was one of their cars. Behind him was a back-up car. Far ahead, he could make out the two cars that bore Simons and his team. They had not stayed in room 1024 for long. Lucas had only just gotten back to the lobby when he saw them marching from the lift towards the door. The whole cars had left almost at the same time.

The car ahead trafficated right and took a side road. The other one followed. A few other cars turned right, including the three CIA cars. They all kept their distance. The first car ahead slowed down about 600 meters from where Lucas' car was. The three CIA cars slowed down to a crawl. After about one minute, they saw that the other cars ahead had stopped. They pulled their cars from the road, and got out. Cars flashed past, their tail lights and head lamps illuminating the darkness.

After a quick consultation the party separated into the two, got into the bush and walked silently towards the direction of the parked cars. They did not have long to walk before they came to a fairly large clearing with a wooden building in the middle. They could make out two guards silhouetted in front of the building. Security was light because the men of the consortium were sure of their plans.

The CIA agents fanned out and half circled the building, from the door of which showed a small patch of light. Without any waste of time Lucas gave the order and feint "phut" was heard from about three sides. The escaping gas darts made for the fired men. They dropped flat on the ground. The men rushed the building and flattened themselves at the wooden wall.

Lucas and the other agents could hear a distinct conversation coming from the building. "Mr. Avalanche wants us to get everything from you before the departure," one of the men inside said. Lucas heard Simons say sullenly: "I've told you everything I know. When are we to leave?" "Soon, soon enough," the man said and laughed mechanically. "Now," Lucas whispered. The men stepped back and crashed the flimsy door open, shooting in the air as they tumbled inside the room.

"Hold it," Lucas said in his crouching position, pointing his gun at the three men that encircled Simons. One of them stupidly reached for his gun. Lucas shot him low in the chest. He fell forward and flattened out. The other two placed their hands over their head. Then without warning, one of the men took a springing run in a flash of second and crashed out of the window.

While Lucas rapt Simons and the other man put under surveillance, crash of gun shots came out of the darkness. There was a yelp of pain and a flurry of movements. Then more gun shots came.

"Welcome back to the company, Mr. Simons," Lucas said. "Did my disguise fool you?" At the sound of his voice, Simons slipped down his chair in a faint, his body twitching spasmodically. There was a sound of running feet. Two agents came to the door panting.

"He escaped," they gasped. "He took about five bullets in his body, yet he made away."

"Did you search everywhere?" Lucas asked.

"Yes."

"We wait a while. He won't get far. Post some men outside." The men left the room in a hurry.

* * *

The wounded man gasped for breath. His hand was bloodied. So was his entire body. With difficulty he got out his cellular phone, flicked his lighter and began to dial. He suddenly coughed, blood trickling down his chin.

"Avalanche, Avalanche," he said when he got through. "They have gotten grass. I don't have much time to live." His body slumped forward and he died facing the ground with the phone in his hand.

At the other end, Jack Edmonds looked around him angrily. He still had the telephone in his hand. Then, he began to dial.

"Falcon, contact Santus immediately," he said after a pause. "Tell him to marshall all the forces. The plan has been activated. We can't afford to lose twice. He breathed deeply when he broke off the connection a far away look in his eyes.

Chapter Twenty

Lerec's countless hours of toil and sleepless nights seemed to have paid off. Since the murder of Guttingberg he had decided that it would pay him to track down the enemy within or at least expose the source of the leak than pursue the still shadowy men of the drug cartel. His reasoning was very simple: of what use was an information he gathered which would be turned against him? Rather than that, he preferred to expose immediately the dangerous leak somewhere in his government; a leak which has rendered useless all his calculations and endangered his life in the bargain.

Now, he had narrowed down his area of search to just two people, and the implication of that was quite frightening for the stability of his government. Never before since the OAS men contracted the faceless Jackal to assassinate President Charles de Gaul in 1 963* had the French Government and security apparatus been so penetrated by the enemies of the state. For the principal suspects in Lerec's mind were the French Minister for National Security and the Chief of Security at the Palace de Elysee. These are the two men, apart from those he had already eliminated from his list, who were constantly briefed about the progress of the investigation.

When his attempt to tap their telephones had failed to reveal anything worthwhile, he had devised another more practical strategy. He succeeded in getting their Chief Security Guards to feign sickness and had planted his own special agents on them. He was now waiting patiently for the storm he knew would break, and he knew that he hadn't long to wait. The palace de Elysee Security Chief was still in Paris, and going by his protocol arrangements, was not expected to travel out of the capital for at least six weeks. Jean Jacques D'Atmand, on his own part had been in Nice for the past eight days and was expected back in Paris in three days' time. Lerec knew that between the two gentlemen, something terrible had happened to the confidentiality of national security information and the mystery behind the bizarre episode would soon be unravelled. He could afford to wait. So, he waited.

About two weeks earlier, just before Simons was taken by Lucas and the men of the CIA, Jack Edmonds had call Barbara Alumineza and given her some briefing. 'The time has come," he said "when our collective desire will be actualized. We've had several set backs and cannot afford to waste time. But before we mae a move, we must have as much information about the opposition as we can manage. It's therefore absolutely necessary that you arrange a rendezvous with Jean Jacques. I understand that he will be travelling to Nice in a few days' time. So many things have already happened since you met him last. I'm sure he will be loaded."

"I'll do my best," Babara Alumineza replied.

"Fine; Let's get to work." Together, with arms linked, they walked from the wooded countryside back to the country house somewhere in the Scottish Mountains that Edmonds had bought a few years back. The sun was setting, throwing up large orange glow when they eventually got to the front steps of the old castle.

* * *

Nice was as beautiful as ever. The sea splashed on the beaches where thousands of vacationers had gathered, to ease stress. The casinos, nightclubs and the other spots that made Nice attractive were in. The sun was up as usual and very reluctant to set even at the approach of night. The streets were busy and gaily dressed people thronged the side walks and curbs, sight-seeing and enjoying themselves as best they could with the facilities which one of the world's most equipped holiday resorts was endowed with.

Jean Jacques had left the beach a long time ago. He had a meeting to attend somewhere in the outer reaches of Nice, so he left Barbara Alurnineza at the beach and went to his Hotel accommodation overlooking the beach. He had just driven off a few minutes ago with one of his bodyguards, the old reliable he had had for quite some years now. The new replacement was hovering somewhere in the beach area, keeping an eye on Barbara. He hoped that his chief bodyguard would recover quickly from the attack of pneumonia that had suddenly laid him low.

Barbara lay on a beach towel, her face turned to the sun, and soaking both its warmth and the sea breeze that fanned her face and the sand around her. She had on a large pair of goggles that shaded a significant part of her face. She got up from the towel and put on her beach wrap. Then she began to go towards the hotel, unmindful of the lustful glances passed at her by the men at the beach. The bodyguard followed at a sedate pace behind her, blending well with the mass of humanity that milled around the beach.

Back at the hotel, Barbara entered the lift together with the bodyguard who kept a deadpan expression. They said nothing to each other throughout the ride in the lift. "They walked down the length of the passage again in silence.

"That will be Alex," Barbara told the guard, when they reached Jean Jacques' room. "I'll be needing you in two hours' time." She smiled sweetly at him, fluttering her eyelashes. Alex bowed slightly, turned back and began walking down the passage towards the lift. He turned slightly in time to see her enter the room. He rushed back to the door and heard the lock turn and the key taken away. He smiled. That would save him enormous problem if his suspicion turned out to be right.

Lerec had briefed him thoroughly. "We do not think that D'Atmand is a traitor. Rather, we feel that somebody very close to him must be working for the Cartel, a mistress or house help probably, but somebody with access to his bedroom and briefcase. We want the person very fast and don't care how you do that."
Alex nodded understandingly. He had been with D'Atmand for over two weeks now and nothing suspicious had come up. It was true that Barbara had been with them for over a week now but she never had the opportunity of being alone herself. If she was their quarry, now was the time to prove that.

He bent low towards the keyhole and peeped into the room. The passage was empty of people but he knew that he had only a couple of seconds before people will begin to appear. He could see that Barbara had pulled out D'Atmand's suitcase unto the bed and was going through some documents inside it methodically.

As she opened her purse to bring something out, Alex fished out a long piece of slender metal from his trousers' pocket, inserted it into the keyhole, fiddled for a short while and then pushed the door open. 'Barbara heard the sound of the opening door and whirled around - she saw herself facing the short barrel of a silencer gun held steady by Alex. She gave a chocking rob and backed away with her hands over her mouth and her eyes staring wide open.

Alex closed the door and chained it in one flowing motion still covering Barbara with his gun.

"Take it easy," he said. "Keep your hands still."

"I am only looking for my personal document he has in his case. He asked me to take it when he was leaving for his meeting."

"That I understand," Alex continued. "Just keep still. We will sort everything out in a moment." He advanced slowly towards her, till he was near her and could perceive her perfume.

"Did you place that thing on the ceiling?" he asked sharply in an agitated voice. Instinctively, Barbara turned her face up at the ceiling to see whatever it was. The corner of her head served a perfect target. Alex slid the gun till he was holding it by the barrel. He smashed the butt on her head, not so hard as to crack her skull; just hard enough to cause her to slump forward and down to the rugged floor in a faint.

He walked over her and reached for the telephone. He called D'Atmand at his meeting place and told him briefly what had happened. He did not wait to hear more from the panicky and agitated minister who appeared very close to collapsing. He broke the connection and called a Paris number.

"I have her in his room," he told Lerec, when he came to the line. Caught her in the act. Everything is as I met it. I've alerted D'Atmand. What should I do next?'

"Just stay where you are. Don't make any move. Say nothing to D'Atmand when he does get back no matter what he says. I will be right over in a chartered jet. Good work," and he hung up.

* * *

For two days Simons refused to talk. The idea of ending it all crossed his mind briefly but he discarded it. It was easy to think that he would take his life when a situation like this ever developed, but when the reality stared him in the face it was something e[se. He now discovered how valuable his life was to him and resolved to take whatever they meted out to him, including trial for high treason.

The press smelt a big story behind the shoot-out in Miami and the secret interpretation of what government officials gave out as a drug baron back to Washington D.C. They were not fooled but they were as yet unable to unravel the mystery behind the situation. There was a lot of speculation but little substance in what they wrote but they continued digging, for a break somehow or the other.

On the third day, the government decided to stop treating him like a top government official and started looking at him like a common criminal. It was this decision, including the hostile attitude adopted by his interrogators that warned him that he will gain nothing by keeping mum. He decided to give them just enough to make them happy and spare him any personal torture but insufficient so that they would still consider him a valuable witness.

He claimed to have been black-mailed by the consortium because of something terrible to did -something strictly personal. They had threatened to tell his superiors about it if he failed to co-operate. That information would have ended his career and ruined his marriage, he only revealed the name of the leader of the consortium as Avalanche, a man of indeterminate nationality. He further said that the consortium had political ambition and had mapped out a strategy to take over the world. He finally corroborated Anthony Roberts' views about the penetration of the American financial network by the consortium and admitted that he worked hand in hand with Roberts who he said has another blackmail victim.

The American government was still deliberating on what to do with Simons when Lucas received the news of Barbara Alimneza's arrest. D'Atmand was forced to resign and the stink could not be hidden from the press which though not knowing the true details nevertheless went to town with the little they had with fanfare.

Barbara broke secrecy and gave more concrete information about the consortium, its leadership and activities. But try as much as they could, the whole of European and American security and intelligence network could not trace the whereabouts of the leaders of the consortium nor locate their headquarters. They seemed to have vanished from the face of the earth; they simply disappeared out of sight. The waiting game, Lucas concluded was on. It behooved the opposition to make the first move. This he knew they would make before long.

Chapter Twenty-One

President Nuka Chiba now had the complete report on the re-organisation and restructuring of the NDA which Tupa prepared. He marvelled at the man's attention to professional details and was glad that such an officer was directly in charge of such a highly sensitive organ of government. He had already approved the relocation of the agency from the Ministry of Internal Affairs to the presidency. The Internal Affairs Minister was clearly unhappy about the situation but he had learnt to accept what he cannot change. Efforts were already being made to practicalise the relocation and before long the agency will be permanently situated very close to his office - a situation he had always desired.

Tupa's report was very comprehensive and it dwelt at length on the local drugs scene, the international links of the local drug barons, the moral, social and medical damage done by drugs and the increasing political consciousness and ambition of the major drug cartels. Though Tupa had not heard of the existence of the consortium, he nevertheless included in his report his belief that the drug cartels were becoming impatient with the international conspiracy against them and may likely shift their focus to the conquest of political power as a pre-condition for the survival of their nefarious trade.

Nuka Chiba underlined that portion of the report, nodding several times as he did. The report also stated that most of the local drug barons are in the trade for the immense wealth it provided since they were essentially apolitical. That explained the existence of powerful cartels in the country. The only group, according to Tupa, known to have extensive internal connections was that led by America, "Tobby Boy" and "Lord Mickey". They were highly connected and even moved around with police protection. It was Tupa's view that one way of arresting the expansion of the drugs trade was the extermination of that group through the incarceration of its core leadership. It will send a powerful signal to the other barons and their influential backers in and outside of government.

President Chiba also underlined that section of the report. The other details were purely of a technical nature. He glossed over them without making any comments. Tupa will handle all that, he answered. His business was to provide the resources and materials to help him achieve that.

He sat back on his chair, satisfied that it had not been a wasted effort. He wondered why he had suddenly become obsessed with the problem of hard drugs of late. Then, the revelation came to him like a divinely sent prophetic message: the whole of mankind was gripped by the trauma of disorders caused by the intake of hard drugs and there were people out there whose principal business was the production and supply of these drugs. Many societies had been ruined by this social, moral and medical malady and several others were already on the verge of becoming huge lunatic asylums, with their major cities becoming havens of mindless violence and unspeakable decay fuelled by the unsatiable appetite of the drug addicts.

'Supposing,' he reasoned, 'these barons were to band together and attempt (even succeed) in seizing political power in some of these countries and derived a new world order based in their warped sense of value? Where would mankind stand? What will be the fate of Africa and his beloved country?' All these questions bothered him of late and he resolved that he must do what he could to salvage his society, and from the ashes of mankind's present decade, make it the beacon of hope for all Africans, and ultimately, for the whole of humanity.

It was a battle worth fighting for, an ideal worth committing resources to, he assured himself rocking forward and backward in his swivel chair.

* * *

The party was welt in progress at the exclusive Paradise Club. It was America's birthday and he wanted to celebrate it in grand style. Tobby Boy, Lord Mickey and the other major dealers were all present.

The guest list was specially prepared and "unknown quantities' were turned back at the gate by stern-looking guards.

Music boomed and drinks abounded. The dance hail was packed to capacity. The party was steadily degenerating into one huge horse-plays but nobody cared. Most of the guests were flashily dressed either in Western or traditional Nigerian wears, though the greater percentage of the girls spotted the briefest of mini skirts and skiing pants.

Outside, the night was hot and close. People walked past the club and occasionally glanced at the shadowy movements inside. Cars passed occasionally, it was 2.30 am and the night was still young for many of the nightclubbers, particularly as it was a Saturday.

Then without warning, a number of small and heavy vehicles roared down the Street and then came to a stop and a few of the passers-by saw several police cars and jeeps pull up.

Tens, of special squad policemen jumped down the vehicles and made f or the nightclub. They carried hand cuffs and pistols. A few shots were fired in the air and the loud arguments by the guards ended in sobbing whimpers.

The revolving glass doors of the nightclub were pushed wide open. Four policemen leant their bodies on the open doors and dim Lights spilled out of the club to the threshold. The music, drinking and dancing stopped. Most of the guests, especially the women cringed away at the sight of the determined policemen.

"What the hell is going on, America shouted, striding to the nearest policeman?" Have you forgotten your manners? A mere phone call will send all of you out of the force. Do you know who you are embarrassing?"

The policeman waited till he was very close to him, and then flexing his muscles, hit him savagely on the face with his gun barrel. His mouth and cheek tore open and a few teeth fell out. He stumbled forward. He rolled over on the floor, moaning. A few of his friends seemed to want to come to his aid. Rapid shots were fired at the ceiling which brought broken light bulbs down.

"Who else wants to be a hero?" one of the policemen asked. "Let him come forward."

The raid was over in a few minutes. The clubbers were all led but to the waiting vans and chained in twos. They glared murderously at the policemen but nevertheless went with them. A few of the girls were either crying opening or sobbing quietly.

* * *

America broke down under torture and told all he knew. He not only gave details which led to the arrest of several other drug barons and thousands of couriers and street dealers, but also ended the career and freedom of a number of top government officials. For the first time since the drug business became news the press halted the efforts of the government and urged it to continue with its war against the trade in narcotics.

An interesting development in the episode was that those names whom Tupa wanted removed from the NDA were killed, almost to the last man, with those whom America and the other drug barons fingered in their confessions. For the first time in recent months Nuka Chiba breathed a sigh of relief, convinced that though the battle had not been totally won, the enemy had, at least, been beaten. He had no illusions about what he was up against and the need to apply more pressure in getting all the necessary information about drug trafficking from the detained barons and the few others still at large.

It was precisely a month after the storming of the Paradise Club that Chiba sent for Tupa. The necessary organisational and personnel changes had been made at the NDA and it had already moved to the presidency. More staff were recruited and sophisticated equipment purchased. Funding was adequately taken care of while the agency had become overnight became a bright spot in a nation whose institutions were riddled with incompetence and corruption.

The discussion took place in Chiba's office. Tupa had become more confident and relaxed in the presence of his president and now walked with an air of purposefulness and self-assurance. He was still aware that most of those who hated his guts were still influential in the government and were only waiting for him to make a mistake and suffer for it. He was also aware that they saw his present romance with the president as a temporary one and that he would soon fall out of favour. He was under no illusions about the sensitive nature of his position, but was determined to do everything to survive for as long as he cared.

Chiba wasted no time in coming to the point. He laid down the paper he was reading when Tupa entered his office and adjusted his spectacles. "Sit down, Tupa," he said when Tupa had greeted him. Tupa sat down, alert and attentive.

"There are still a lot to be done," Chiba began. "We have only scourged the threat; not destroyed it. You are aware that Nigeria is only a transit station in the global drugs trade. That the nation neither produces nor consumes in any commercial quantity most of these drugs."

"I know that Sir," Tupa replied, nodding his head.

"Well, then," Chiba continued. "If you know that, you will also know the local drugs trade would not thrive without the support and encouragement of the international drug replacements for those already apprehended, establish new routes and networks and make new contacts."

"That is possible Sir. Not only possible, Sir, but practicable," Tupa added.

"The Americans are encouraged by our efforts so far arid they want to show their appreciation. They are inviting the leaders of our anti-drugs agency to the United States to visit the new anti-drugs outfit they have established. You will leave for the United States in two weeks' time. Choose two other men you think will profit from this trip."

"Thank you Sir," Tupa said. "That will be all". Tupa stood up and made his way to the door. Lest I forget," Chiba added. "The Americans pretended that it's just a routine visit; normal stuff. But it's not. They are up their neck in trouble with the drugs chaps over there. They feel that something is about to happen; something terrible. I want you to be there when it does happen; I want one of my men to be there when it begins. May be you will have an interesting story to tell me when you get back; who knows.

Chapter Twenty-Two

The Take Over

It was a quiet July morning in Bogota. The sun shone brightly on the paved streets. Bogota had awaken from a night of tropical restlessness and unfashionable fears. People went about their normal business, unmindful of the usual power-play that went on in the capital. Vehicles clogged the narrow streets and roads, blared their horns and raised hell. Hawkers went about, determined to make two ends meet before the ferocious mid-day sun set in. So, also were the street urchins and pickpockets who knew that morning period was the best time to operate as the dustbins would be full and fresh and people's wallets still full.

Inside the presidential building, an emergency meeting of the cabinet was already in session. The Colombian president sat at the end of the long table. Behind him were a few of his trusted aides and assistants. Flanking him were, his cabinet ministers most of whom came with their special assistants. These stood quietly behind their bosses.

There was only one subject on the agenda: drug trafficking. The activities of the cartels had picked up after a lull which followed the killing of Pablo Escobar. Now they were not just back to normal; they were in fact, getting out of hand. And the pressure was mounting from the USA for a major, determined and sustained crack down on the drug cartels. The demand by America was accompanied by a veiled threat of withdrawing military assistance, and scrapping a number of bilateral agreements that favoured Colombia.

The president was determined to respond to the American initiative and had summoned his cabinet to find ways to, at least, curtail drastically the exploding trade on narcotics. His Army Chief, Chief of National Security and Chief of the Police Department all waited in a room just behind his chair. They would be summoned at the appropriate time to present their reports and proffer opinion on the problem at hand.

Suddenly, there was a flurry of movements in the heavily

guarded presidential palace. Loud shouts were heard and the sound of running feet echoed sharply on the marbled corridors. Hundreds of voices were raised in songs of protest about the menace of the drug barons and government's inattention to the security needs of the people.

The president paused in his address and glanced at the men around him. "What could that be?" he asked nobody in particular.

"There are voices singing outside and the guards seem to be arguing with them," one of the ministers said. "Let me go out and see."

What he saw when he stepped outside was baffling.

Hundreds of peasants were gathered outside the gates of the presidential palace. The vehicles that brought them, ostensibly from remote villages and far-flung districts were just behind them. They had placards and were demanding to present their petition to the president.

Most of the guards clustered around them; and those who were not calming them down were very relaxed, amused by such a scene.

Their attention was totally directed at the events at the gate. As the minister summoned one of the few guards near the building to give him a message, the sky over the palace suddenly went dusky with the explosion of several smoke bombs. They seemed to be fired from long rocket launchers. As the smoke spiralled upwards creating an eclipse-like halo over the building, the sound of helicopters were heard nearby. About twenty of them menaced the palace ground and the men aboard began shooting as they descended.

The scene at the gate took a dramatic turn. The peasants scattered in all directions, making way for some of the vehicles which had been driven close to the gates. Heavy rockets were fired from the vehicles, tearing the gates apart and killing some of the guards. The other guards moved back only to encounter more firing from the men alighting from the helicopters. Vehicles drove inside the compound, and from the rolled down windows turrets of heavy machine guns were seen, firing steadily. Three helicopters landed on the roof of the building and some of its inmates lowered themselves to the ground with ropes that had spiked ends. There was chaos in and outside the building. The president and his men were paralysed with shock. Before their brains could function properly, and before commands were issued to open the doors to the underground tunnels, the door burst open and men wearing gasmasks entered the room. It was soon all over. Most members of the cabinet were either killed, wounded or captured. The president was led away in cuffs to one of the helicopters. Though commands were issued to the nearby military cantonment, it came too late. By then, the presidential palace was completely in the hands of the invaders.

The only other sign that showed that the take-over was complete was the sound of artillery fire which came from the direction of the radio and television Stations. It ended after about fifteen minutes. Then there was silence. The voice that came on air one hour later was polished and its message brought a temporary halt to life in the capital and the other major cities. By nightfall, an announcement was made that most of the military formations had fallen to the new leaders who will name their cabinet the following day.

* * *

In Bollora the take over was equally dramatic; The Radio and Television stations fell a little after 12 midnight on the same day that the Colombian presidential palace fell. The dispirited and poorly motivated soldiers staged only a perfunctory resistance and capitulated to the superior fire power of the invading forces. Thirty minutes after the invasion and after the news came that the president of the republic had been captured, the radio came on air again, announcing at half-hourly interval, the message of the new leaders.

It was a message that caused confusion and consternation among the law-abiding segments of the populace and struck fear into the hearts of all anti-drugs agents. It was a message of a new order to run solely on the parameters set by the consortium.

The following morning, the streets, stores, shops, cafes, offices, market places and public squares were completely deserted to the columns of menacing armed guards who patrolled either on foot or in convoys of vehicles. Sporadic gunshots were heard at intervals.

By evening, the whole country had been pacified and the new rulers had virtually settled down to the business of governance. It was Roberto De Silva, a notorious drugs baron wanted in Bolivia, the USA and various other European countries, that emerged as the acting president of the republic.

Apart from Colombia and Bolivia, some of the other nations of South America suffered similar fate. However, there was a stalemate in Peru and Panama and a couple of the other obscure islands. Those other nations tottered on the brink of civil war and collapse as the struggle for political power between the old leaders and members of the consortium escalated. Everyday brought tales of horror as entire cities and villages were attacked by rampaging hordes of insatiable marauders.

The situation in Asia was less gloomy though the fall of Thailand was a mortal blow to the foundation of the old society. After marshalling their forces for weeks from the Golden Triangle, forces which were strengthened by new recruits from Burma, Malaysia, Singapore and bands of renegades from the other South East Asian countries, the consortium attacked Bangkok and brought the government to its knees. Before nightfall, on the third day of heavy fighting, the consortium succeeded in establishing its power in virtually all parts of the country. From there too issued proclamations which altered the general direction of society and established a new social contract based on the power of narcotics. Kazakhastan and Afghanistan, two principal routes in the Asian drugs business also fell to the drug barons. By that singular success, the consortium could lay claim to a global leadership spread apart from the yet to be violated European and North American states. As nation after nation fell, new routes and border posts were drawn on the basis, not of territorial integrity and sovereignty of existing states, but on the merchantilist and commercial whims of the drugs merchants. As many inter-state divisions crumbled, they were replaced by an emergent logic of a new world where boundaries and divisions were marked by the need of trade and profit.

* * *

The whole world was in a state of shock. Newshounds were at their best with sensational reports of unfolding events. Global Television and News Networks interrupted their programmes to give an up-to-date information about the escalating situation. Others devoted their programmes entirely to the offensive of the drugs consortium.

An emergency special session of the Security Council of the UN was convened and apart from the usual diplomatic representation at such a session, the governments of the USA, France, Britain, Russia and China sent their Foreign Ministers to the meeting.

Though the delegates resolved on a whole number of issues, and took concrete steps to beef up the defence requirements of collapse-prone Asian and South American nations, there was a lingering feeling that they had left it too late. They could take the overthrow of some of the nations in their stride, but they knew the security consequences of the capitulation of the government of Kazakhastan. This was because apart from Russia and Ukraine, Kazakhastan haboured the deadliest of the former Soviet Union's nuclear stockpile including the ICBMS, SLBMS, MIRV's and special nuclear-tipped rockets. The meeting, therefore, ended on a somber note and the weary delegates hurried away unable to evolve a strategy capable of stopping "these mad men" from pressing the nuclear button.

* * *

The US president summoned a meeting of the National Security Council. Joe Lucas was invited to testify. Though he was repeatedly pressured and threatened to reveal the name of the leader of the consortium, he refused to be intimidated. He merely stated that he suspected who the leader was, going by certain things Anthony Roberts and Simons said; and based on the information his field men had been bringing of late. He assured them that he would be able to tell in a few days' time and that contingency arrangements should be made because he may move on a very short notice

141

against the imposter. The meeting ended on that note.

* * *

Lerec rummaged through volumes of papers and files till the early hours of the morning. He still had thousands of reports to wade through and wondered whether he stilt had enough time to do that. He was getting closer to the source of the whole mess, and the more he dug, the more convinced he was that he would soon crack the case. He reminded himself that he would call Lucas the following morning. It was about time again, they got together, he told himself.

* * *

Jack Edmonds raised his glass of champagne in the dim light. "To the revolution," he murmured. "To the revolution," those around him said. Together with Edmonds, the entire members of the high command were present. They were celebrating their victory so far. "Two more Asian and European nations to go," Edmonds said, "and we will be ready for the USA. Uncle Sam will have no choice. There is always Kazakhastan to equalize things." He laughed heartily and took a sip of his drinks.

Chapter Twenty-Three

Joe Lucas developed an immediate liking for Tupa. He spent several hours explaining to Tupa the functioning of the agency and the steps they had so far taken in order to arrest the drift into chaos. Though Tupa came from a background that lacked technical sophistication and international anti-drugs experience, Lucas quickly learnt to trust his intelligence and power of observation. He saw through the man's transparent honesty and eagerness not only to learn but also to impart what little he had to the operational strategy of the American global network.

Several things had happened simultaneously. Lerec had visited from Paris and together they had pierced all they knew about the leader of the consortium. They had now come to the Conclusion that the American Jack Edmonds, international financier, respected whealer-dealer and globe-trotting businessman was the dangerous leader of the dreaded consortium. They had already passed this information to the governments of the USA, France and the other major European nations.

But such knowledge did not simplify the task at hand. Lucas knew that Edmonds was as slippery as the eel and tracking him down now, especially as he had several countries he could now enter as a lord, was a very difficult task. He analysed in his mind all that they knew about Edmonds and an image of a chameleon came to his mind; a man capable of disappearing on the shortest possible notice without a trace; a man who so hid his true identity for over fifteen years and deceived the wittiest in the world's business circles with ease; and a man who combined an intriguing and very sophisticated business and financial prowess with the organisations acumen that produced the hydra-headed consortium.

He dismissed the thought that Edmonds would be operating out of one of the countries his consortium had already taken over. Nothing in his dossier pointed to that. Visit, yes, but not a permanent habitation. Those countries, excepting the strategic importance of Kazakhastan, represented but the marginal elements in Edmonds' global thinking and Lucas was certain that the man thought globally.

Where then would he be and what were the options open to him? What would his first move be? When had he decided to show his hand for as yet, he and his group had not claimed any special responsibility for the recent earth-shaking events apart from the fact that known drug barons were heading the governments of those countries where the change had occurred?

These were some of the questions that bothered Lucas as he set about preparing his men for an assignment that would be as dangerous as it would be sensitive. The American agency will provide the bulk of the men, about twenty. France will produce Lerec and four of his most reliable and trusted assistants. The rest of Europe will provide four. Asia and Latin America, that were still spared the scourge of the consortium will provide four, while Tupa of Nigeria and Zhukov of Russia will complete the team.

He had been rehearsing his men for over one week now and was convinced that they would make their move in a couple of days. He had his own hunch about where Edmonds would be but was hesitant to rush things. He would take his time in this particular case, and with such a man probably having the key to the Kazakhastan nuclear strategy, there would not be a second chance.

* * *

A few days before Lucas and Lerec decided to make their move, Tupa cabled the following message to president Nuka Chiba:

Greetings from the USA.

You were right once again, Sir. The whole place is agog with activities and the fear of the unknown still hangs over the leaders. I've been made part of the new team that will stop this madness before it gets out of control. We are almost set to go. Had you not moved the time you did, our beloved country would have been in the same mess that so many others are in now. How I wish that other African leaders will emulate you. If they do that our continent's condition will not be that hopeless. I will keep you posted as we make progress, though everything will now take place in the field.

Good bye, Sir.

Chiba read the message again and again, and his face lit up with contentment. He proceeded to file it away in a special folder that he normally took to his house at the close of the day's work. He will study it again that night, he promised himself, line by line and word by word, he promised himself.

From the wooden hunting-lodge in the wooded mountains, Jack Edmonds prepared his final time-table for the take-over of the globe. The new regimes he put in power had all consolidated. There was not one case of reserval. Rather, a few other countries were ready to go. His men under the capable military leadership of Dos Santus only awaited his order. He had decided to hit the West where it would hurt most. After the take-over of a choice European nation, he would then announce his presence and his new social, ethical, political and economic blueprint for humanity. He missed most of his lieutenants who were no more, particularly the ravishing Barbara Alumineza. His face darkened at the thought of her. 'Godspeed, my angel,' he thought about her, 'they can no longer stop us now. No matter what they have done or do to you, you are already part of the new world order.' He thought once more about Kazakhastan. He would be visiting there soon, after his latest offensive. Once there, the world will remember that he ever existed. He poked the crackling logs of wood in the fire place, and the now blazing fire illuminated his animated face.

* * *

Two days to the beginning of the operation he was about to mount, Joe Lucas assembled his 30-odd men at the CIA control room in Langley and gave them their final briefing. Tupa was among them. Like the rest, he was gripped by intense excitement with a touch of uneasiness. He was the only African so selected to participate in this global effort and was proud to have that distinction. He felt that he was part of a history-making team; a team that was poised to maintain the human balance in favour of sanity and recognized norms of proper behaviour and social conduct.

Lucas was at the table at the far end of the fairly large room with Lerec and the CIA director Chris Williams. Behind them was an overblown map of the world which was illuminated by computer-controlled lights. In front of them were the assembled men who sat on padded benches. A few of the men had note pads and other writing materials.

"What we are about to do," Lucas said, standing up and walking closer to the men, "is a proper touch-and-go operation. Its high risk nature need not be over-stressed. We're dealing with insane men who wouldn't hesitate to use nuclear facilities against the rest of mankind. They are desperate and know that time is running out for them. Mistakes must be avoided at all costs. And the only way to achieve this is to be as cautious as possible."

He paused for breath and watched the men's attentive faces. Then, he walked to the blackboard on which hung the world map. He picked a long aluminum stick whose tip was equally illuminated by glowing light.

"Our operation will begin on the evening of the day after tomorrow," he resumed, holding the stick in his two hands. "The first team comprising ten men will be air-dropped at a distance of seven kilometers from the location of the opposition. That will be at the lowest range of the nearest mountain." He pointed at a section of the map from where a blush light glowed on and off.

"They will make their way towards the wooden mountain lodge at a North-East direction, passing through the thinnest part of the dense forest." He traced their movement with the stick whose illuminated tip pin-pointed positions that glowed on and off the map. There was absolute silence in the room. Chris Williams sat with his jaw propped up by his hands. Lerec was turned half-way so that he could watch the men and at the same time watch what Lucas was doing on the backboard. The rest of the men sat still, hardly moving.

"They will stop at exactly this location which the satellite photographs have shown to be steep and undulating. That will be after about half an hour of steady walk." He pointed at the location, a small blown out area that was circled by bright blush light.

"The next batch of ten men will move under-water till they are within three kilometers of the lodge at the opposite side of the mountain. They will break surface at 1 9.30 hours on the dot and their wears will blend with the environment. They will make their way through this route," - he traced the route on the map -"till they are about half a kilometer away from the lodge. Some of the men wrote briskly on their note pads, noting the essential points he had made.

"The remaining ten men who have the toughest part of the job will dress like picnickers. They will be made up of five men and five women and will have all the necessary camping equipment they need. They will drive up this mountain road," - this he pointed out on the map - "passing through small villages on their way till they are within two kilometers of the track road that leads to the lodge. Our information reveals that the first line of ruined approaches and sentries are located at approximately less than half a kilometer to the lodge. This group will be intercepted."

He paused again and placed the stick on the table. "This is where the operation really begins. One of two things will happen when they are intercepted. They will either be marched to the lodge for trespassing or be herded off gruffly and told to get back from whence they came as the property is a private one. It's important that they are not herded away. The only way to achieve this will be to make a hell of an innocent noise about their right and the fact that they will not leave till they see the owner of the property. But they have to be careful how they do this, as the men may be under pressure and trigger happy. Assuming that they have their way, they will be led, under surveillance to the lodge where they will be detained till the following morning, presumably. The time it will take them to argue and eventually get to the lodge will be the time the parachute team would have gotten to about 314 metres of the camp and the under-water group at approximately the same distance. If the~ campers create the necessary diversion most of the guards will be attracted to the scene. This will give the other two groups the necessary opportunity to move very fast."

Lucas sat down and held a whispered conversation with Lerec and Williams. He straightened up again and looked at the men and women facing him soberly. "Ladies and gentlemen," he said, "the rest is for you to decide. Nobody can predict how the operation will progress beyond this point. But no matter what you do, know that the fate of mankind lies in our hands, and that the future of our civilization will depend on how you accomplish this mission. Lerec and myself and about three others will be in a high-flying sub-sonic jet watching the events below. We will make our drop at precisely 22.40 hours; that is about three and half hours after the commencement of the "real" operation. The implication of that statement was not lost on the people present. If they slip up, fail in their duties or leave anything undone, they will be placing the lives of their leaders in grievous danger. It's like an ultimatum, no retreat, no surrender. It brought them sharply to the reality of the task ahead and its significance to the existence of the world.

"Any questions?" Lucas asked. There were none. "There will be a rehearsal of what has just been stated. Nobody should decamp under any condition whatsoever." The men and women began to file out one after another. A few talked in low tones. Lucas, Lerec and Williams stayed back to iron out a few things. Outside, the sun shone brilliantly, creating bright patterns on the gardens and lawns that verged the control room.

* * *

"What is the possibility that this lodge may have been discovered?" Jack Edmonds asked those present in the sitting-room. They were about nine in number, three being ladies.

"None whatsoever," Escravor Odaja replied, sipping brandy from a frosted glass. We are as safe as we can be. We could be here for the next ten years and nobody will be wiser about our existence."

"Nevertheless, have the guards beefed up," Edmonds said. "They have to be on absolute alert till we make our move. Friedreich, check out the helicopters again this evening, and make sure that they have enough fuel for the first leg of our trip. We move in three days' time." The others nodded.

"When we get to Kazakhastan", Edmonds added, "I'll issue the thrust in the series of the new proclamations. That will serve as the first warning shot about what is to come. The next three proclamations will determine the new universal order. After that, there will not be any going back for us and for them. We have accepted their challenge. Soon, they will know what stuff we are made of." The men and women nodded again in silent appreciation of the truth of his statement.

Chapter Twenty-Four

The forest was unusually very quiet that night. Rain had been falling steadily a couple of hours back accompanied by the ominous crash of thunder. But now the rain had ceased, the thunder stilled and the intermittent flash of lighting reduced to a barely visible dazzle. The trees dripped water gently to the ground. Streams ran in several places, making soft gurgling noise as they carried along with them broken stems, dry leaves and other pieces of forest rubbish. Far in the North-West side, the sea lay still though occasionally its water lugged gently at the shore line.

Two groups of men and women were positioned at different directions of the wooden hunting-lodge. Some crouched on the ground, their ears cocked for the slightest noise. Others leant on tree trunks, pressing their bodies close to the trees. The night was starless and the forest was dense and echoing. The darkness did not bother the men and women because they wore night glasses, electronically controlled visual aids which radiated ultra-violent rays. They could distinguish between the trees, creepers and the narrow forest path.

Faintly in the distance, they could hear the whispered conversation of the guards and the patter of their feet as they trod on rotten wood. Occasionally, there was a high pitched laughter and the men talked excitedly about the picnicking party they had intercepted and the joy the ravishing five women with them would given them for the night.

The plan had gone very well. The under-water party had gotten to their location without being detected. They had journeyed on land for over three kilometers and now they were at a distance of less than five hundred meters from the lodge, very close to the first line of mined fences and the very related guards.

The group that headed for the mountains from the North-East direction had also gotten very close to the lodge and with the under-water group, formed a fairly formidable semi-circle around the lodge. Only the entrance to the lodge was exposed; the entrance through which the party of ten picnickers was marched to its backyard about two and half hours earlier.

That adventure had taken place successfully. The guards who intercepted them were gruff and angry with them for straying into a private property. They explained that their vehicle had broken down a kilometer away and they decided to explore the neighbourhood in search of help; that when the rain started, they decided to explore further deep in the woods if they might find an abandoned lodge to shelter them for the night.

None of these explanations impressed the guards who demanded that they leave the vicinity and go back to where they came from. The group resisted this, partly pleading for understanding and partly insisting on their freedom of movement. Exasperated, the chief security guard ordered that their rusack be searched thoroughly. The search revealed only canned food, toiletries, clothes, talking ropes and some books. The talking ropes were taken away and the rusack ordered to be repacked. No weapons were found on any member of the party because they were safely concealed in flush bottoms and sides. Bodily searches also revealed nothing. The chief guard then decided that it would be wise to march the party to the camp where their leaders would take a decision on the detainees. Moreover, the female detainees were not bad-looking at all, and the night would be wet, lonely and cold. Chuckling, he directed his men about what to do and the whole party was marched to the hunting lodge. No decision was taken that night for the leader of the consortium felt that the best thing was to detain them till the following morning or even the day after tomorrow when they would be set to go. It would be risky sending them away for the night because they were bound to find one of the out-laying villages where they would spend the night and tell tales of well armed guards on an isolated mountain lodge. Inside and all around the hunting lodge, activities were on top gear. Guards were also inside the thick woods, armed with light machine guns and bayonets. They kept a sharp look-out for other trespassers and anybody foolish enough to stray to that part of the forest.

In the sitting-room of the lodge, Jack Edmonds was holding

discussions with members of the consortium's high command. He was explaining to them his proposed time-table for the remaining part of their operations. The movement to Kazakhastan, he stressed, would make a turning-point in their career. That would be done by him, Odaga and the French man D'Armee. The others would journey by designated routes to the various countries they now controlled. Signals had also been received, he informed them, about the beginning of the Spanish and Burmese operation. That would come precisely a week after his departure to Kazakhastan. Two weeks from then, he would issue the first proclamation and then order for the assassination of the president of the USA, the British Prime Minister and the French president. Their men had already taken positions and were waiting for directives to be issued. The successful prosecution of that part of the operation will signal the beginning of the new universal order. In the midst of the confusion created by those events, select American and European cities would suffer from nuclear blast. Thereafter, the whole world would capitulate to their aggression.

"Brilliant, brilliant," Odaja cried out reaching for a glass of brandy. He had been drinking steadily since the rain started, and though he was not exactly drunk, he was far from being sober.

Edmonds glanced at him from the corner of his eyes. Odaja was alright, he thought, but he drank a lot. 'There would be time to take care of that,' he reasoned. 'No point in denying the man the right to the happiness he had worked for.'

Suddenly, there was a flurry of movements from outside. Several guards ran past and the night was split with the sound of gun-shots. Instructions were issued hurriedly. Odaja staggered to his feet, picked his loaded revolver from the table and went towards the door.

"Find out what is happening," Edmonds called to him. "Let me know soon enough."

"What the hell is going on?" Odaja screamed when he was outside. He summoned one of the guards who ran to him excitedly.

The others were still firing at a particular direction of the forest, the flashes from the gun lighting up the dark night.

"The trespassers have escaped," the man gasped. "They stabbed three of the guards with daggers they brought, and before we knew it, they ran into the bush." He pointed at a particular direction of the forest. "Two other guards are down," the man continued, "they shot them low. The others are in hot pursuit of them."

"Stay where you are," Odaja ordered him, "and tell those crossing you to go back to their original positions. This could be a trap." The man nodded dumbly as Odaja rushed inside the house again.

"Could be a trap or could be that the trespassers got desperate. They may have thought that their end has come. They stabbed three of the guards and shot two others. They escaped to the forest with our men in pursuit."

"I smell a rat in this," Edmonds said simply. "Get ready all of you. You know what to do." As they began to leave the room, the night came alive again with more explosions. Men yelped in pain.

The explosions seemed to be coming from three different directions. A large orange ball of fire was seen a short distance away. Without being told, Edmonds knew that somebody had exploded a bomb inside one of the special helicopters. Another explosion occurred on the South-West side and another of the helicopters went up in flames.

The gunshots were now ominously close. The guards were steadily pressed back. Figures darted in and out of the bushes and close growing trees and it was difficult to distinguish who was who. Edmonds went into the inner room of the lodge, closely followed by Odaja, D'Armee and the others. There were three women with them. Somebody blew out the candle lights and flashed a bright torch.

Suitcases were drawn out from under the bed and sent down to the soft ground through a low window that had been partly opened. Then the men and women began to jump down through the window. Edmonds was in the middle. He cursed steadily and incessantly and was consumed with rage. 'What could have gone wrong?' he thought. 'So these bastards knew that we are here,' he told himself angrily. He would have made his move a long time ago but hesitated at the last minute. He was not in panic but he knew that his task was now doubly difficult and dangerous.

As they darted to the outer edges of the forest, two heavy helicopters seemed to have taken off from nowhere and heading for the building. Their lights were on full blast. Gunshots went up the air. The forest was awash with light. The building made a perfect target. The helicopters came very close to the clearing, dipping here and there to avoid the bullets. Then, they released their rockets at the building. It burst into flames, further illuminating the forest and exposing the location of the guards.

Some of the guards now ran about in panic and were promptly picked off by the invaders. Edmonds and his group crashed inside the forest making their way desperately to the last of the concealed helicopters. A hand grenade was lobbed inside the bush and fell very close to the last members of the fleeing team. Its exploding sound reverberated all over the ground. Four men and a woman were caught in the blast. They threw their hands up and fell with a thud to the ground. The others quietly disappeared into the dark night.

The two helicopters circled over the burning building for a while and began a fast descent. As they touched the ground, the men aboard them alighted. Tupa who was part of the squad that attacked the lodge initially saw Lucas and Lerec get out of the helicopters with the members of their team. They moved forward to welcome them.

The fighting had died down considerably. Only occasional sniper shots could be heard and the sound made by the arms of their men mopping up the remaining guards. The men and women clustered around the jet and listened as Lucas and Lerec briefed them. Others kept watch, their vision sharp and steady behind their unusual glasses.

Lucas was about to give the order for the identification of corpses scattered all over the place and for emergency medical attention to be extended to the wounded when a whirring sound caught his attention. The lodge and its immediate vicinity were awash with bright light which the two helicopters provided. He pricked his ears and signalled to the men to stop talking. Occasional gunshots came from the distance and a few forest animals darted through the branches.

Above all these, he could hear the distinct sound of a helicopter engine coming alive. He rushed to his own helicopter and instructed the pilot to start the engine. Lerec dashed into the other helicopter and gave similar instructions. The other men kept watch below, alert for any suspicious movement.

As the blades of the two helicopters started rotating, they saw another helicopter lift off the ground somewhere in the middle of the forest and began to gain altitude.

"Take off immediately" Lucas shouted to the pilot and keep close to it." The two helicopters lifted of f the ground and rushed towards the departing one. The helicopter in which Lucas was, outflanked it on the left while the one Lerec flew outflanked it on the right. The chase was brief and dramatic. The two helicopters converged on it above the still sea. The two pilots beamed instructions to the pilot of the fleeing chopper to land. Rather than doing that, it gained speed and began a zig-zag movement over the sea. The two USA special forces craft soon covered the distance. Two other instructions were given which were not acknowledged. Then, the inevitable happened. Both helicopters released their rockets which were aimed directly at the rear of the fleeing one. The explosion was deafening. The helicopter caught fire. Having lost control of the stricken plane, the pilot hastily opened the cockpit and ejected into the water. The plane continued nose-diving till it hit the water with a hissing splash. Then, it began to sink, steadily, chumming water all around it and throwing sprays of water above.

Epilogue

Jack Edmonds' body was never found. The bodies of Escravor Odaja and D'Amee were recovered before the break of dawn the next day. For two whole weeks, deep sea divers searched for miles on end but there was no sign of the body of the leader of the consortium. Not even his clothes were seen nor any personal effects. It was as if he was not in the helicopter, or if he was, that he had vanished without a trace.

Another speculation soon emerged that the flight of the helicopter was merely a decoy as Edmonds never was in it. It was even assumed that he lay for the whole night in the forest and then made good his escape at the approach of dawn. The whole forest area, within a fifty kilometer radius was subjected to an unprecedented forest man-hunt, yet, it proved unsuccessful. His photograph was circulated within the same length of space but it yielded nothing. So were the radio and TV broadcasts that offered an incredible reward for anybody who had information that could lead to his arrest.

Gradually, the hunt lost its steam and he was presumed to have been eaten by the sharks in the sea into which the helicopter had plunged. The disappearance of Edmonds weakened the power of the consortium and caused its eventual disintegration into numerous competing cartels and alliances. Not even the rumour that he had been sighted in Kazakhastan could bring the magic back. For before long, popular patriotic forces overthrew the wayward regime and declared the rural, political, social and economic affinity of the new republic to the rest of the world. In the other parts of the world, the consortium lost ground as nation after nation threw off their crippling shackles and formed new regimes that opposed the drugs trade.

Joe Lucas retired from active service to a small New Mexican village where he became a high school teacher. Thoughts of even getting married, raising children and settling down even occurred to him. Lerec also left the secret service and bought a small, but well maintained olive farm where he planned to spend the rest of his life. Tupa returned to Nigeria to a triumphant reception and was awarded the nation's second highest honour. Soon after, several delegations came from different African countries requesting that President Nuka Chiba should loan him out to them to establish their own anti-drugs agency. Both Anthony Roberts and Simons were convicted for high treason and were sentenced to life imprisonment in a New York's most notorious penitentiary. For all intents and purposes, life seemed to be going on normally. The sun shone in the mornings and afternoon and night came at its usual time in the same repetitive rhythm.

* * *

The America president was not amused by all these events. He was rather frightened about the reality which the threat of the consortium had fore-grounded. He had always thought that the drugs business was a marginal, though lucrative economic activity that lacked the competence to threaten the fabric of their society's social existence. Now, he knew better. Anthony Roberts' and Simons' confessions, shocked and rattled him. Going by their disclosures, he may have to set up judicial panels in virtually all government agencies and institutions which had had dealings with drug barons. That, of course, was impossible.

A few bad eggs would have to go, but the deep seated contamination of American social and economic life by the drugs business seemed permanent and even irreversible.

He commissioned a team of experts, drawn across wide-ranging inter-disciplinary fields at the height of the confrontation to investigate the effect of the drugs trade on American life and social system. The report was submitted just yesterday and the first few pages did add grey hairs to his head and caused a sharp increase in his blood pressure.

He now clutched the report he had forced himself to read three times and stared out of one of the bay windows that lent his office its distinctive character and colour. Sweat dripped off his face to his neck and collar in an endless stream and his hands were clammy. He wondered if the statistics contained in the report were real and reluctantly agreed that the experts had done their job.

His mind flashed across the images that presented themselves to the nation at intervals on the national television. A man ran berserk, walked into a crowded cafe and shot ten people dead. Crazed youths roamed inner city streets, marching, lapping and killing innocent people. Teenage girls jumped off sky scrappers to their death. Mental homes became over-crowded by deranged inmates who stared blankly into space. High school children shot their colleagues and teachers at random on the least provocation. The list was endless.

Behind most of these atrocities, lay the sceptre of narcotics. It was the death of their civilization, he thought. Drugs could well be the cause of their national decline. Then, the idea came to him as if by transcendental epiphany: no civilization in all recorded history had actually collapsed in the face of external aggression. It was always internal decay. Greece, Rome, Persia, etc. went that way. Any factor or a combination of factors always made it so. In their own case, he reasoned, it was hard drugs.

His mind went to a future in which his entire nation may become one large asylum populated by irredeemable junkies, deranged by narcotics. Then, moral conduct will collapse, only to be replaced by a state of national degeneracy. With that will come the inevitable death kneel of his proud and great nation.

'God forbid 1' he almost shouted out, laying the report on the desk and gripping the chair's arm-rests with a violent possessiveness. 'It would never happen,' he consoled himself. Drugs will not bring the death of America. America will always win its war against her numerous enemies. But such thoughts may be in vain as the new inheritors of the universe will be those nations whose poverty had made them producers of narcotics or become its marginal consumers. Only they may have the moral purity and strength to dwell in the millennium to come. Yes, nations in places like Africa and elsewhere will.

The idea stabbed him like a crude dagger to the midriff and he got up from his chair. Then weighed down by the enormity of his thoughts, he groped his way wearily to the door without a backward glance at the report that still lay solemn on his well polished desk.

Printed in the United Kingdom
by Lightning Source UK Ltd.
1392